MEGAN MULRY

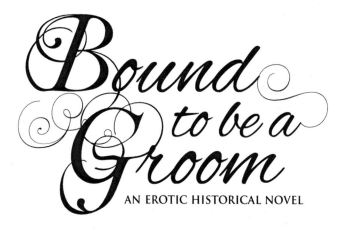

AN EROTIC HISTORICAL NOVEL

RIPTIDE
PUBLISHING

Riptide Publishing
PO Box 6652
Hillsborough, NJ 08844
www.riptidepublishing.com

Bound to Be a Groom

Cover Art by L.C. Chase, lcchase.com/design.htm
Editor: Sarah Frantz
Layout: L.C. Chase, lcchase.com/design.htm

ISBN: 978-1-62649-113-7

First edition
April, 2014

Also available in ebook:
ISBN:978-1-62649-112-0

MEGAN MULRY

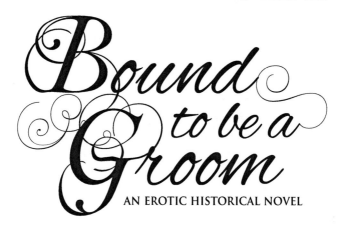

Bound to be a Groom

AN EROTIC HISTORICAL NOVEL

RIPTIDE
PUBLISHING

TABLE OF Contents

Badajoz, Spain – June 1808

Anna Redondo was unaccustomed to feeling at a disadvantage. It was not in her nature. She knew she'd been born on the wrong side of the blanket, but that had never prevented her from knowing her own mind. Having spent her first eighteen years within the walls of a convent might have limited her experience, but it had not curtailed her imagination.

And she could imagine all sorts of things with this man.

Regrettably, imagining would only take her so far; she needed to act. Taking a fortifying breath, she turned to face him.

"It's going to be quite a long afternoon for those two, don't you think?" she ventured, gesturing toward the bride and groom. Isabella and Javier were walking at the front of the wedding party with the bright morning sun, so particular to this part of southern Spain, glinting off the beautiful silks and polished leather of the aristocratic guests all around them.

"Pardon me?" Sebastian de Montizon asked, clearly surprised at the audacity of a polite young miss speaking to him so directly.

"They look miserable, don't you think?" Anna mused. She had left the convent in Burgos two weeks ago and traveled to Badajoz in a carriage, chaperoned by one of the older nuns. Apparently, the short time away had already emboldened her.

Sebastian stared down at her as they walked, assessing her through hooded eyes while the *clank* and *clop* of horses and regal hardware around them seemed to fade. "I think they look blissfully happy. Whatever do you mean?"

But she suspected he knew what she meant and was only pretending to be confused by the demure front. "Of course they're happy to be married," she said brightly, then, in a lower voice, "but now they have to wait and wait until they can be alone . . . on their wedding night . . ."

Over the past week, dignitaries and aristocrats from all parts of Spain and Portugal, and even a few from France and England, had filed into Badajoz. Sebastian had swept into the main hall shortly before supper three days ago, looking like he had spent the past month splitting his time between a bar and a brothel. His dark hair had been too long even by today's liberal standards, and the scruff of his beard had looked untended. For the wedding, he had reacquainted himself with his valet, and he now looked like many of the other perfectly turned-out aristocrats. But there was still a look of something wild about him.

Anna's first thought upon seeing him had been that he needed to be taken in hand . . . and that she'd be the one to do it.

"What do you know of wedding nights, little convent girl?" He smiled and stood straighter as he kept walking alongside her through the winding cobbled streets. He clasped his strong hands confidently behind his back, as if he'd assessed her and seen all he needed to see of the little flower.

Perfect. Think of me like that.

"Nothing firsthand, of course. Only what I've imagined."

That got his attention.

"Imagined?" His voice cracked.

She smiled at the small victory. Anna needed experience, and here was a man who obviously had it. She assumed he would be discreet—he was a devoted and loyal friend of Javier de la Mina, her friend's new husband—so he wouldn't betray Anna's secrets. In short, he would suit.

Sebastian continued to look at her, and she felt her cheeks flush. The slightest narrowing of his eyes told her the rising color pleased him.

"I have a very vivid imagination," she whispered with throaty promise. She licked her lower lip, tipping her face away from his, hoping it was just enough to make him want to dip his head to look longer. "And I know how it feels to postpone my own desire." Finding her pace, she sallied forth into his stunned silence. "I think once you feel something, it's easier to discern in others." She paused for effect. "Do you agree?"

When he nearly stumbled on a cobblestone she feared she'd gone too far. Neither she nor Pia had any experience with men, of course, but they'd convinced themselves that if they could make each other shudder and beg, surely a brutish man would succumb to far less.

It appeared they had been quite right. Sebastian looked as if he were about to make love to her reticule as it bounced back and forth against the apex of her thighs with each of her steps.

She held it slightly away from her body. "Do you fancy my reticule?"

His eyes flew up to hers.

Spectacular eyes, she had to confess. They were just like Pia's—that familiar greenish blue that made her think of the Caribbean Sea and the places the two of them had dreamt of spending their future. Places like Cartagena or Hispaniola, where she and Pia would live a quiet life of spinsterhood, disguising their passion for one another behind practical worsted dresses and massive studded doors that hid all manner of things.

"Such eyes . . ." She hadn't meant to say it aloud, but the color reminded her so much of Pia. Regardless, Sebastian seemed to enjoy the attention. *Useful information*, she thought. *He likes to be noticed.*

His smile encouraged her to go on admiring him. It should have been irritating that he wanted his ego stroked—that such a gorgeous man seemed to crave endless praise—but Anna found it endearing. She was surprised to realize how much she liked the idea of Sebastian softening under her care, bending to her will. She wanted to stroke him.

"The blue of your eyes reminds me of—" She hesitated, then continued more carefully. "—places in the New World, places I've heard of but never seen."

He looked interested then, and not merely in the flush of her cheeks or the moisture of her plump lower lip. "I was on my way there . . . before this transpired." He said the last with an impatient toss of his gloved hand in the general direction of the bride and groom. She admired the way the kidskin molded to his strong fingers.

"Your hand is quite something, as well," she said in a slightly rougher voice.

He smiled again, turning his hand this way and that, as if he'd never before taken a moment to look at it. "Really? I have two in fact." He presented his left hand as evidence, then lifted his right forearm for her to rest her hand upon. "May I escort you into the *alcázar*, Lady Anna?"

"I'm no lady, I'm afraid. A lowly miss."

He kept his arm extended. "The offer still stands . . . my dear Anna."

And there it was. *My.* For a few minutes or hours or days, she would be his. He had knowledge and experience.

She needed both.

She placed her gloved hand on the fine fabric of his dark-green jacket, lightly at first, then with a grip borne of excitement as his muscles flexed and shifted beneath her fingertips. She was loath to admit that the low, throbbing heat between her legs was not entirely the result of conjuring her passion for Pia.

Chapter 2

His eyes came to rest on her lower lip, wet from her constant back-and-forth nervous licking with the tip of her tongue. "Do stop that, please," he begged.

But she didn't stop. She only paused for a moment, and instead of withdrawing that flicking little pink tip, she challenged him with her eyes. The flare of her audacity sent fire into his blood. She opened her lips wider and let her tongue drag a leisurely circle around the entire red, wet opening.

He did stumble that time.

Sebastian was no longer deceived by all that virginal frailty—that impossibly elegant neck with the birthmark at the base near the lacy edge of her gown, the arms and legs that moved like delicate damselfly wings. "I see you use a convent education and a pale dress to disguise yourself, much as I use a family name and a sword."

Her eyes widened at his brash speech, but she didn't reply.

"I know what it is to live behind a mask, Anna."

He also knew what rested behind her careful shell: something hot and honest and demanding.

The man he presented to the world was the strong, strapping soldier; the agile, competent horseman; the eldest son of a powerful landowner; the heir being groomed to follow in his father's illustrious footsteps; even the rebellious rogue. Not one of them was the real man, the lover who craved nothing more than to be completely subdued by a powerful, knowing partner. Or two. To be taken in hand and made to fulfill every outrageous need, to experience the freedom he only found in submission.

He must have sighed at the thought as he looked ahead to the castle in the near distance.

Anna squeezed his arm to get his attention. "Perhaps the two of us shall find one another behind the mask, then?" she offered.

He took his time meeting her gaze, letting his eyes slowly caress the turn of her bodice. Her breasts were small, but he saw them respond to his consideration, two firm, puckering tips forming beneath the pale silk as he rudely stared. If he could please her with a look, he could only begin to imagine how he might please her with his fingers or lips.

When their eyes met, he was certain she knew the nature and extent of his thoughts. "I should like that very much," he replied softly.

Their intimate conversation had slowed their pace somewhat, but they were nigh on the castle walls when one of his friends jabbed his ribs as he passed. "Step lively, Seb. Don't want to hinder the lady."

This was no lady, he wanted to call after his mate. This was a hidden world of sensual delight, his for the plucking.

"Where did you learn to do that with your tongue?" His voice was rough around the edges, hard from repressing the urge to drop to his knees and burrow under her gown right there in the shadow of the castle's portcullis.

She smiled, tightening her lips around her teeth, then spoke with that soft convent voice he was coming to recognize as another subtle layer of her nuanced disguise. "I'm sorry. My lips . . . they tingle sometimes, and it helps to . . . soothe them." She tested the theory, letting her tongue pass slowly across her upper lip. "Yes. It makes them feel better somehow."

Enough. Enough about tongues and desire and soothing the tingling feelings or some such rot. He hustled her into the castle along with the sea of other guests.

He knew the layout of the *alcázar* from several visits in his childhood. Guiding Anna gently away from the masses of people, down a separate hallway, as if he were innocently leading her to a view of the mountains from a particularly scenic balcony, he turned the black wrought iron handle on a heavy wooden door and pulled her inside.

Victory.

He shut the door behind him and peeled off his gloves. The two of them were in a vast library with thousands of volumes and nary a human in sight.

"Do it again, please," he asked. "With your tongue." Slowly untying the silk ribbon of her bonnet, Sebastian let his knuckles trail along her milky skin as he spoke. She was distracted by the grandeur of the room, marveling at the countless books.

"I've never seen anything like it," she whispered.

"Neither have I," he agreed, touching the sensitive edge of her lower lip with two fingers.

She gasped briefly and looked so genuinely surprised by his touch that he faltered. "You can't possibly play the blushing virgin now . . . after you . . ." But he didn't move his fingers, and she didn't pull away. Her dark-amber eyes were now fixed on his.

Then she did the most miraculous thing imaginable. She opened her mouth wider and drew his bare fingers into that wet, succulent warmth. Her eyes were still wide for a moment, but then they fluttered closed in sensual delight. She worked his fingers with her mouth, letting her tongue swirl and lick as she sucked and moaned.

He could have come from that—from looking at the way her cheeks drew in and from her guttural moans vibrating from the tips of his fingers to the throbbing tip of his cock.

"Good God, woman!"

She emerged from her temporary reverie—eyes glassy, lips wet—and slowly withdrew his fingers from her mouth. She still held on to his wrist with both her small hands. She'd grabbed him in that way at some point in her ecstasy, controlling his pace in and out of her mouth.

"Did it feel as nice for you?" she asked, almost innocent.

He shook his head in stunned disbelief. She was an angel from heaven. From some carnal heaven, he amended, that produced an angel born wanting to suck a man's cock for the sheer pleasure it brought *her*.

"Yes," he croaked, then cleared his throat. "It felt very nice."

"For me too," she said, but she released him and wandered away toward the endless shelves of hand-tooled leather, as if her enjoyment of the act had been somewhat unexpected, something to be examined rather than indulged.

Sebastian followed her. That in itself was remarkable. He could not recall willingly following a woman. In bed, of course—more than willingly—but not like this. Anna was a lady, no matter how lowly a *miss* she claimed to be, and it was as if his two distinct worlds were colliding. Social obligation and base desire were finally making one another's acquaintance, like two people who turn a corner and hurtle into each other.

She was trailing her fingertips lightly across the bindings of a complete set of Shakespeare.

"So you can read, I take it?" He came up behind her and circled her waist with his arms. She leaned back into him, but again, it was almost absently, as if he offered a convenient perch for her to use while she perused the library. Nothing more. The idea pleased him, the idea of making it his purpose in life to be of *use* to this woman.

"I can. I love to read." Her finger came to rest on *The Tempest*. "But I've had very little access to . . . so many things."

Chapter 3

She turned in his arms, staring into those blue-green eyes of his, wondering how honest she could afford to be. Some version of the truth would free her to ask all sorts of relevant questions, to make him an accomplice of sorts. He seemed like he'd be game.

"Sebastian..." They'd been properly introduced, but it was wholly improper for her to call him by his first name. Then again, she was already alone with him, unchaperoned, having recently lost herself in the sensation of sucking his fingers until her sex was throbbing so hard she'd forgotten her own name. Calling him by his Christian name did not seem to sit quite so high on the long list of improprieties. What with one thing and another.

"Yeeessss..." he drawled. He'd begun swaying her gently in his arms, as if they were on the deck of a slow-rolling ship.

"I..." She hesitated and then cursed her unfamiliar cowardice. He was quite right in letting her know she couldn't very well play the blushing virgin when she'd more or less lured him into their current embrace. He was staring at her mouth again—making love to her mouth with his eyes, really—which made it easier to blurt out a portion of the truth. "I would very much like to... do things... with... to... I would..." *Well, this is going abominably.*

He smiled and kept up that gentle motion, pulling her nearer with each sway. "That all sounds positively delightful," he said, "but perhaps a bit vague."

"Vague?" she prompted.

He inhaled. "I tend to prefer very clear directions." He was quite close by then. In fact, the hard pressure of his cock was resting against her stomach at that very moment.

"You do?" she asked, surprised and delighted at her good fortune.

He nodded and then looked adorably sheepish as he pressed his length along her belly.

I can do this, she thought.

He felt big, but certainly no bigger than anything she and Pia had used to penetrate one another. Fingers at first. Then tongues. Then more fingers. Anna's whole hand one time, after much patient, delectable coaxing. Anna felt the heat pool in her belly at the memory, at the way their shared desire had ultimately opened Pia up to her so completely.

She closed her eyes, overcome with memories.

Abbey of Santa María la Real de Las Huelgas, Burgos, Spain – September 1807

Initially, they had tried to ignore the heat that flamed between them. For many months in the spring and summer, they would catch one another's eyes and quickly look away—in vespers, in the library, at mealtimes. They would speak of art and nature and herbal remedies, books and political ideas and astronomy . . . but never of feelings.

Anna had tried to quash her feelings through petition and penance, with prayers for forgiveness and relief from her agitation. She had tried to deny how deeply she loved Pia, to convince herself that she only loved her as a friend. She had tried to persuade herself that her physical desire was part of a childish infatuation or sinful temptation, a brief flare of unfamiliar lust that would pass soon enough.

But it hadn't passed. It had grown.

So, when she began to suspect that Pia felt the same way, there was nothing for it. Anna finally decided to declare her feelings one warm afternoon in September, when the two of them were sent to the surrounding forest to collect some late-summer herbs that would be dried during the long winter. Pia appeared serious and thoughtful as always, but Anna's heart thudded wildly, emboldened by their exceptional solitude. The novices were rarely granted times to speak privately, so Anna saw it as an opportunity to dash her foolish hopes. Perhaps she had imagined Pia's answering gazes, and Pia would put an end to her madness once and for all.

"Do you look forward to spending your life in the convent, Pia?" Anna tried to sound casual as she bent to snip an herb.

Pia turned her head slightly. "I never think about it one way or another. It will be my life whether I look forward to it or not."

Her moderate, equable nature was something Anna had come to love about Pia because it was the shell she wanted to break apart, to see what roiled beneath.

Choosing her words carefully, Anna said, "I think about it." *I think about taking you away with me.*

Bending to pick a stalk of malva, Pia spoke without looking up. "As well you should. That is your future, is it not? To be a lady-in-waiting at court next year?"

Anna couldn't look away from the turn of Pia's long back and strong shoulders. She could stare at her for hours. She was desperate to touch her. Her breath caught in her throat.

"Anna?" Pia was standing in front of her by then, stepping closer.

"Yes?" She licked her lips in the one nervous gesture she'd never been able to conquer.

Pia looked at her mouth for a split second. "Are you unwell?"

"I don't know . . ." Anna whispered, her heart pounding.

"What is it?" Pia's voice had softened to a near whisper, as well.

Anna gathered all her courage. "I believe I'm in love with you."

Pia didn't gasp or step back, as Anna had half hoped she would. They stood like that in the dappled glade—staring at one another—until the autumn noises of the forest were like clanging cymbals all around them. Insects skittered and dried leaves crackled into the air. An acorn falling might as well have been a hundred-year-old oak crashing to the earth for how the small sound resonated.

Finally, after what felt like an entire rotation of the moon, Pia's eyes blinked slowly, then drifted shut. The sparsely filled basket slid out of her weak hold. "Touch me," Pia pleaded. "I beg you."

That was all the encouragement Anna needed. Within seconds, she had pinned Pia against one of the large oak trees. After so many months of wondering and hoping, the reality of Pia's lips and skin and hair threw Anna into a sort of frenzy. Kissing her lips and then along the strong turn of her ivory neck, nipping at her ear, Anna reveled in the physical reality of Pia in her arms. The smell of her—a mixture of fresh autumn air and spices from the convent kitchen where Pia had baked bread that morning. The sound of her—a loving compilation of supplication and devotion.

Anna began removing Pia's clothes without asking permission, pulling desperately at her tightly wound coil of hair. The more Anna pushed, the more Pia bent. As if they were both perfectly attuned to the moment and its meaning: that they were both discovering their true natures. Pia was made to soften and sway into Anna's controlling, greedy hands.

"You are so beautiful, Pia, so strong and wise," Anna gasped between kisses and fumbling fingers. "I watch you all the time, how you manage everyone without flouting the abbess's authority." Her lips trailed down Pia's neck. "I've seen your lovely drawings and your modesty about them. I've seen your patience with the younger girls. I love watching you."

"I've watched you too, Anna," Pia confessed, her breath shallow. "I've watched you grow into this woman who knows her own mind. I see how you look at the world. How you will take what you want."

"I will take you. I know that now." Anna's voice was low and demanding, and she watched as Pia's body responded to its strength—her strength. "My wild ideas about you have become so real to me." Pia whimpered at the words, and Anna kissed her full on the lips, savoring the texture and taste, the feel of Pia's tongue against hers.

Anna broke away for a moment. Pia leaned her forehead against hers and said, "I've dreamt of you so many times, Anna." She reached tentatively to hold a strand of Anna's silky blonde hair between her curious fingers. "You come to me at night, into my bed, like an angel."

Anna laughed, low and mischievous. "If I am an angel, I'm an angel of darkness." She spoke as she worked, removing the last of Pia's clothes with rough, tugging movements. Every time she gave a firm pull at a piece of fabric, Pia seemed to come emotionally, as well as physically, undone. "The thoughts I have about you, Pia, they are dark and heathenish. Beautiful and raw."

Chapter 4

"Oh God," Pia whispered after Anna removed her coarse overdress and her well-worn underclothes. All that remained was the long skein of linen that Pia used to bind her large breasts. She had never been naked in front of anyone. Out of fear or habit, she reached up quickly to prevent Anna from removing the last vestige of her modesty.

A stormy look of disapproval passed across Anna's face, and she took a step away from Pia. Many years later, when Pia would look back over the course of their life together, Pia knew this for what it was: the first small punishment for her defiance. At the time, Pia was confused, both timid and exhilarated at once.

"Don't ever do that again," Anna said, in a gritty voice that Pia felt in the deepest parts of her throbbing body.

Pia had spent her entire life in the convent, where her very existence had been defined by obedience; this felt like something else altogether.

"Drop your hands and open yourself to me, Pia."

The submission Anna was demanding of her was something far more complex—far more rewarding—than the monotonous conformity of her daily life. Anna's voice elicited a kind of sensual obedience that required strenuous complicity, not complaisance. A shiver ran down Pia's spine.

"Do you like when I tell you what I want?" Anna trailed a single finger along Pia's neck. "When I am firm with you?"

Pia nodded, almost weeping with the truth of it.

Anna held her chin. "Answer me, my sweet. So I know you feel it, too. I want to hear your gentle voice crack under the weight of it."

"Yes, Anna . . . I love when you speak to me thus." Pia gave herself to Anna in that moment, gave herself into the other woman's keeping. With her head tilted back against the rough bark of the tree and her hands hanging loosely at her sides, Pia arched slightly forward, offering herself to Anna. It was as if they had become one in mind and spirit before they had even begun to explore one another's flesh.

"Remove the binding, my love." Anna's hands grazed over the linen where it was pulled tight and firm across Pia's breasts. "Slowly."

Pia wanted to do as she was told. Resolved, but with trembling fingers, she began to unravel the fabric from around her ribs. She feared her heart was unraveling right along with it and hoped Anna was not orchestrating their mutual destruction. The possibility was distinct, if not deterring.

When the fabric pooled at her feet, near the overturned basket, Pia didn't know what to do with her hands. Seeking something to ground her, she reached her hands behind her and let the rough bark of the tree dig into her palms, as if she were tying herself to the mast and Anna was the siren.

Her heart pounded madly as Anna stepped closer and said, "You are the most gorgeous creature, my wild forest nymph."

Pia arched her chest closer to Anna's outstretched hand, her body begging for contact. "Please, please, please touch me."

When Anna's small delicate hand finally caressed the bare skin of Pia's breast, they both stopped breathing. Pia's eyes were heavy with desire, an unfamiliar thick warmth that pounded through her veins and prickled her skin.

"Pia . . . I want to do so many things . . . with you . . . to make you feel . . ." Anna pinched Pia's nipple and watched as her skin tightened in response.

Pia could do nothing but gasp.

Then Anna looked down at the thatch of black hair between Pia's legs. "Do you touch yourself here?" Anna reached with her other hand and cupped Pia's mound before she could answer. The sensation was explosive and grounding all at once. The physical contact of Anna's hand pressing against her most private self—imprinting Anna's ownership upon her body—had Pia shuddering as if she'd been struck. A seeking finger slipping into her moist channel had her crying out. Anna's assault was a declaration that Pia was hers—as if she were silently asserting, *These breasts, this moist heat: mine.* It was a consummation.

"Yes," Pia confessed, her voice reedy. "At night. When I think of you. I tried to stop, but when I imagine you—" Pia gasped again when Anna's finger began to circle her sensitive nub.

"It's torture, isn't it?" Anna asked.

"Mmm hmm." Pia bit her lip at how sweet the torture was, all the sweeter now that it was really Anna's hand and not Pia's imagination.

"Hold on, Pia. Hold on for as long as you can. And then let me take you."

"Yes, Anna . . ." The words floated out of her.

When Anna's lips captured Pia's hard sensitive nipple and her tongue mimicked what her fingers were doing below, Pia wasn't able to contain her reaction. A cry of complete surrender ripped through her. From that moment on, Anna's hands and mouth took complete possession of Pia's body. The hard bark pressing against the flesh of her back contrasted with the press of Anna's soft mouth and demanding hands.

"You are so slick and hot, Pia. So good for me." Anna's narration heightened Pia's response; warm liquid heat slid down her inner thigh. "Ah, you like when I tell you how good you are, don't you?"

Pia nodded helplessly.

"You are *very* good," Anna whispered in her ear as she put a second finger, then a third into Pia's throbbing, swollen sex. "I want to know every inch of this body of yours. I want to make it sing for me."

"Oh God," Pia whispered. "It's coming over me, Anna. I'm going—"

Anna kissed Pia's lips and plunged her tongue into Pia's mouth while she turned her fingers against the sensitive inner walls of Pia's channel.

"Anna! Stop!" she protested against Anna's sensual assault.

But she didn't stop, and Pia was glad. Anna kept stroking that inner place she must know so well from taking her own pleasure. The desperate pleading of Pia's voice only seemed to drive Anna harder to prolong the agonizing pleasure.

"Never," Anna whispered. "I'll never stop loving you." She moved her fingers in and out several more times until Pia was completely spent, the final reverberations of her climax shuddering through her.

Anna kissed Pia more gently, then helped her settle to the ground. She spread out Pia's dress, and they used it as a blanket to rest upon. Anna lay back and pulled Pia's naked body alongside hers, rubbing her bare back in long soothing strokes to warm her skin against the cool air.

When Pia began to come back to herself, her hands started wandering over Anna's slim body. "You are so much better than any dream."

Anna laughed. "I certainly hope so."

Pia blushed. "I meant . . ."

Anna softened and kissed her again. "I know what you meant. I'm sorry to tease. You are so sweet and perfect. So natural. I feel as though you have always been mine."

God, how those words soothed and excited Pia. "I feel it too, as if I have always been preparing for you, to be yours." And there they were: no negotiation, no confusion, only the simple realization that *that* was the nature of their relationship, the fabric of their love for one another. That Pia belonged to Anna.

Chapter 5

*A*nna stared up at the canopy of autumn leaves, her heart more full than she'd ever thought possible. Pia was hers. Then thoughts of the outside world began to crowd up against her as she held Pia close.

"What is it?" Pia asked softly, her fingers lightly tracing the lines of tension in Anna's forehead.

Anna relaxed into her touch and turned to face her. "I don't want you in stolen moments like this. I want you with me all the time. I want us to be together, like man and wife . . ."

Pia looked taken aback, as if Anna had gone mad.

"I mean . . . Ugh. That's not what I mean." Anna shook her head to reorganize her thoughts. "We can never marry in the eyes of the world or the church, of course. I meant I want us to be together as we are now, not furtively."

"I know what you mean." Pia relaxed deeper against her chest. "But we both know such a dream is impossible."

"Nothing's impossible," Anna said with a bit of harshness that seemed to surprise Pia. "I am a planner, not a dreamer."

"I suppose if you were able to stay in the convent, rather than go to court in Madrid, we could be together. Sometimes."

Anna reached out and tenderly fondled Pia's breast. She felt her own sex flutter in response to Pia's immediate reaction. They were already part of each other.

"When it comes to you, my darling Pia, I will never settle for *sometimes*. I have a plan." She leaned down and began kissing Pia's lips and then her neck and then, for quite some time, her breasts, and then lower, until Anna had her mouth against Pia's full, wet center, and she brought her to the heights of pleasure again. And then again.

Anna's own release would come soon enough. Her self-denial was a joy in itself. For that moment, she loved the way Pia melted beneath her touch, the way Pia's hips rose to meet her lips, the way Pia's soul flew into Anna's keeping.

"I will never give you up, Pia. Never." She licked and taunted and nipped at the swollen lips between Pia's legs. She brought her to one last climax and finally relented when Pia's voice was shredded from screaming and her face was covered in tears of ecstasy.

For several months after that, though, they were required to settle for *sometimes*. They planned the occasional clandestine meeting. They carved out a few blessed nights when one of them feigned sickness and the other came to her aid. Pia continued to beg Anna to take what little pleasure they had and be grateful for the crumbs.

But Anna refused to settle for the rest of her life.

Finally, after many weeks of stolen conversations and heated debates, Anna was able to convince Pia that her plan to amass a small fortune—by becoming a courtesan—was the only one that promised a realistic path to an independent future for both of them. Anna hated the idea of leaving Pia in the convent, but Anna's aristocratic—if tainted—blood meant she was destined to live amongst the upper classes, with ready access to the men who would gladly pay for the pleasure of her company. Pia had no such connections, sullied or otherwise.

Occasionally, Anna faltered, wondering if she should take the less treacherous path, if she should accept the measly life the convent offered. But she never let Pia see those doubts. One of them needed to be unequivocally strong, and that role suited Anna far better than it suited Pia. When their last night together was upon them, the night before Anna was set to leave for the wedding in Badajoz, she tried to keep her spirits high for Pia's sake.

"If I'm to become a courtesan in Madrid—or if I'm particularly lucky, perhaps the mistress of a wealthy nobleman in Paris or Naples or London—I'll need more experience, darling." Anna dragged her hands lazily through her lover's long, dark hair, Pia's head resting on her chest.

"I know you do, but I still hate it." Pia's hands roamed across Anna's smooth stomach and then up to one breast. Pia leaned down slightly, taking the pert nipple between her lips.

"Oh, Pia," Anna sighed. "What else am I to do?"

Pia released her breast and expelled an answering sigh. "You could remain here."

"If it was always like this—" Anna squeezed her closer to make her point. "—then of course that would be perfect." The two of them were whispering intimately in the narrow single bed in Anna's sparse room in the convent. "But I shan't spend my life hiding, sneaking around behind the abbess's back, taking a night here or there—like tonight—when one of us pretends to be ill and in need of the other's aid. We deserve to live together, always."

"I know," Pia agreed reluctantly.

"It's a terrible bargain but one we've reasoned through so many times. It's the most expeditious route, don't you agree?"

"Yes, up here." Pia tapped her head. "I know it's the quickest way for both of us to escape, but so much can go wrong. What if you fall in love with someone else?"

"Oh, Pia." Anna leaned down and kissed Pia's forehead lightly, then trailed kisses down her cheek until she reached her mouth. Pia groaned, and her strong body softened and bent into Anna's. "How could that possibly happen? You are everything to me." Anna reached her hand between their bodies and began touching Pia's breasts, pinching and toying with her nipples until Pia was squirming and halfheartedly pleading for her to stop.

Anna and Pia had fallen horribly, madly in love over the past six months. They both knew the night might be their last in each other's arms for many, many months, or even years. The abbess had arranged for Anna to spend several weeks with Isabella in Badajoz, and then Anna was scheduled to travel directly to Madrid to take a position as a lady's maid in the retinue of the off-and-on monarch, King Ferdinand VII.

As they spoke of the future, Anna did her best to hold fast to the last precious moments of the present.

"You must believe me, Pia. I will prevail."

"I trust you," Pia whispered. "I know you can accomplish anything you set your mind to, but it's quite awful for me to imagine you with . . . *under* . . . some horrible man." Pia shut her eyes.

"Perhaps I'll learn something that will please you," Anna teased.

Pia groaned and turned her head into the pillow. "How can you joke at a time like this?" she said into the linen.

Anna sobered. "If it means the two of us will live together eventually, I am willing to do almost anything."

"Oh, Anna." Pia looked up and kissed her again. "I know it's true, but it's still miserable. I know the sooner you are able to accumulate some savings—with the gems and baubles I'm sure every man will shower upon you—the sooner we will be together. Men will fall at your feet. I know it."

"I will always be thinking of you. I will always picture you. No matter what they do to me, it will be your lips and hands and skin that I feel."

Pia was crying again. "I will miss you horribly. Please think of me and know that I am thinking of you."

"I will. Of course I will." Anna's voice was almost stern as she looked down into Pia's moist eyes. Holding Pia's chin firmly in her hand, Anna watched as her lover's sadness turned to beautiful submission once Anna was back in control. It took all of Anna's conviction not to waver. She was sorely tempted to simply give in to that look, the look that fired Anna's blood and made her powerfully aware of what the two of them shared, the look that made Anna feel whole.

"May I show you how much I shall miss you?" Pia whispered, always tentative and painfully shy when she wanted to please Anna.

"Yes, my love. Show me."

Pia worshipped Anna's body, taking slow, reverent care as she kissed her way down Anna's lean frame. She was incredibly patient, protracting every moment of their dwindling time together. She licked Anna's small breasts, and they both moaned when she pulled one firm nipple into her mouth. Anna ran her fingers through Pia's unbound hair and encouraged her with whispered words and humming sounds of pleasure.

When Pia moved lower, she looked up at Anna, wanting both physical and visual contact.

"I see you, my love," Anna whispered. "Go on."

Hesitant and eager, Pia began to slowly lick the seam of Anna's sex. Anna's fingers flexed and then relaxed against the back of Pia's head. "Yes, my sweet girl."

As Pia's eyes closed in submissive pleasure, Anna nearly wept, once again questioning her wild plan. During their time together, Pia had proved to be the most exquisite, delectable lover. She moaned, a combination of carnal satisfaction and bittersweet regret. Pia looked up from between Anna's legs with sadness in her eyes.

"What is it, love?" Anna reached out and touched Pia's moist lower lip.

"Please don't let anyone else do this."

"Men will want to touch me, darling . . ." Anna's voice trailed off, not wanting to hurt Pia but not wanting to promise something impossible, either.

"I know." A single tear trailed down Pia's cheek. "But not with their lips." Her expression veered toward anger. "They'll want to fuck you with their pricks or prod you with their thick fingers. Please . . ." Pia kissed Anna there, then sucked lightly on her clit before speaking again. "Let my mouth be the only one here." Her eyes were begging.

"Very well. Only your mouth will touch me there, sweet Pia."

Pia's eyes drifted shut, and Anna could feel the curve of her smile as she pressed her lips with renewed fervor against the throbbing lips of Anna's sex.

Chapter 6

Badajoz, Spain – June 1808

In the library with Sebastian, Anna tried to conjure the same warmth low in her belly that a look from Pia had always produced and transfer it to this dark-haired, arrogant aristocrat. She hoped to feel even a hint of that kind of passion while he held her in his arms.

Sebastian's length twitched against her, and she felt her desire fade. Unfortunately, the idea of intercourse—or more accurately, penetration—left Anna cold. It was too invasive, too one-sided. Even the words—*fuck . . . prick . . . needle*—sounded inelegant at best and violent at worst. Crude.

Not to mention the possible consequences, which led to ruined lives and unwanted wailing bundles left at convent doors. In addition, she dreaded the way the act itself called for her own nonexistent passivity, to be pinned down and poked. Or at least, that's how it had always seemed to her.

"Come here," Sebastian said, gently drawing her toward a large velvet sofa in the center of the room. He tried to lean her back into a partially reclined position, but she immediately sat upright.

The buttoned front of his straining buckskins was right at eye level. Quite convenient.

Then he touched her—stroking down her neck—and Anna instinctively reached for the fall of his trousers. When she palmed the straining fabric, he gasped, and she snatched back her hand.

"May I?" she asked, looking down, unsure if his shock was physical or a matter of etiquette. She tried to remind herself to be more polite, but the idea that she was about to make these discoveries in broad daylight, with a willing partner, was more than she could have ever hoped for. If she were to arrive in Madrid with a modicum of sexual experience, perhaps she could secure a position as someone's mistress more easily. Still, as much as she wanted to learn what she could from this man, the idea of being his acquiescent pupil was anathema. She wanted to be in charge.

As usual, Pia would have said in that throaty voice of hers that always bordered on a shy laugh when remarking upon Anna's dominance.

He chuckled and folded his arms arrogantly across his chest. "Do with me what you will."

She felt she'd been granted free access to El Escorial, with no pricking or poking in sight. She palmed him through the fabric first, wanting to get a sense of his size and what pleased him, and if she were lucky, what pleased her. In future, she knew her control of a lover would derive from her ability to sense his likes and dislikes, but from her time with Pia she also knew her own pleasure could be equally arousing to her partner.

Sebastian's groan was immediate. She pressed harder, and he pushed his hips toward her. She licked her lips, and the thought popped into her head that this might be entirely delightful.

Keeping one hand firmly against his considerable length, she used the other to undo the surrounding buttons. The front flap came loose, and she slid it down to release his straining cock.

She looked up at him to make sure he was still . . . pleased . . . and the gleam of lust in his eyes assured her he was. She'd been in this position often enough. She loved the feeling of Pia's frantic hands in her hair when Anna kissed and licked and loved her swollen petals. She loved making Pia wait and wait and then break apart—against her demanding lips—only when Anna finally let her.

She wondered aloud, "May I take you into my mouth? Perhaps you'd like to grab hold of my hair . . . or my neck?"

He looked shocked. Probably a result of her forwardness. She was consumed with a spontaneous terror that she had stepped so far beyond the pale that he'd never—

He dug his fingers into the base of her skull, giving her a fierce tug that only granted her a split second to open her mouth and receive his enormous shaft flush up against the back of her throat. She almost gagged, but he pulled back enough for her to breathe through her nose, then, more slowly, he went deeper. Petting her and gently asking her to relax, he trailed his hand along her neck, occasionally dipping the tips of his fingers into the edge of her bodice.

She let him set the pace at first, but she was eager to experiment. She braced her small hands against his bare hips, then trailed them lower until one hand found the base of his cock. She circled it with delicate fingers that barely connected, squeezing once to get a sense of his resilience. He groaned again—a deliciously deep, primitive sound—so she squeezed him harder.

"Oh dear God . . ." His voice sounded almost angry, but she knew it for what it was. Raw pleasure. She worked his cock like she'd worked his fingers—like she worked Pia—at times giving him deep, hard suction and at other times taunting him with featherlight licks, edges of teeth, air.

"Anna . . ." It was a warning of sorts.

Breaking the suction, she said, "No, no. You must be patient. I have so much to learn."

His thighs quivered, and he reached for the back of a nearby chair to keep himself standing.

"That's right," she directed. "Be a good lad and hold on for me . . ." She nodded her approval of his restraint, then dipped back to take him full and hard to the hilt. Her throat was already softer and more relaxed, able to take more of him without resistance. The power she felt at his desperate compliance was beyond anything she could have hoped for.

She found his sac with her other hand and fondled him there as well, learning the feel of the skin and the weight of him. She tried hard and soft pressure, tugging and lightly scratching until she knew what brought him the most pleasure. He liked it rough.

Delighted shivers rippled through her. If he reveled in her coarse treatment, she was thrilled to oblige.

She reached further around. Her hands were already slick with her own saliva and the salty, smooth cum that seemed to be seeping out of him with every pull of her greedy mouth. Their earthy scents and fluids were mixed together. Her nostrils flared with pleasure, and then she pushed her wet index finger against the pucker of his arse.

He cried out, a fierce animal sound that escaped from his beautiful lips before he could repress it.

She released his cock from her mouth, but she kept up the pressure at that intensely sensitive spot, taunting him as she spoke in a near-careless tone. "You like that?" She pushed against his tight hole. Her voice was a throaty purr from having the head of his cock so far down into her.

When he didn't answer, she started to pull her hand away.

"Oh, God, yes! Don't stop . . . please," he begged.

The sight of him at this point of heedless, shameless entreaty thrust her into some glorious place of wanting to ride him hard, to push him to the absolute limits of what he could bear. Her body hummed in anticipation of the liberties she wanted to take with his desperate body.

"I like it when you say *please*." She took him deep again, and his answering moan snapped through her body. With one hand at the base of his cock, she used the other to circle his tight arsehole with two slippery fingers, straining her eyes up to watch the way his face contorted and smoothed in lovely agony.

She wanted to penetrate him. She loved all the ways she could get inside Pia's body—her mouth, her pussy, her arse—all the ways she could devour her and be devoured in return. She wanted to be inside Sebastian in the same way. To reach into him, to grab what she felt was—already, bizarrely—rightfully hers. And then watch him break apart in her hands and explode. She wanted to make that happen, to be the one who made him feel things that no one else had ever made him feel.

Pia always told Anna that she was such a generous lover, but the truth had nothing to do with generosity. Anna was greedy. And arrogant. She knew how to do this. It was as if she had been born for it. She had worried she only had this intuition, this ability to seduce, with a woman's body, Pia's body, because the reaction she could tease and strum from Pia's eager, smooth flesh was nothing short of miraculous.

But Sebastian's responsive enthusiasm was equally delicious. She didn't know him, of course. She certainly didn't love him the way she loved Pia, but the way she made his body dance and sway was quite divine. His pliancy was beautiful.

Without bothering to ask for permission, she circled his arsehole one last time, then pushed her slick fingers inside him right as she drew his cock deeper into her mouth and sucked and bobbed her head. She kept up that pushing and pulling, front and back, in and out, until she felt the hot gush of his release against the back of her throat and the clenching echo of his pulsing climax around her fingers in his arse.

She was cruel, relentlessly prolonging his sweet, convulsive repercussions. She sucked on him harder, swallowed every drop, and then she slowly licked him clean. She suspected he was sensitive, as she always was, as Pia always was, so she became gentler then, but still persistent. She licked him tenderly, circling the base of his softening cock with her tongue to lap up the saliva and semen there. And it was splendid. He was so satisfied, exuding a throbbing energy of pure, satiated bliss.

That she had provided, that she had given and taken from him.

She removed her finger from his arse even more carefully, petting his hip slowly with her free hand as she did. Praising him in some unspoken way.

When she had finished smoothing his shirt back into place and buttoning up his trousers, she finally worked up the courage to look him in the eye. "I think that was a decent start, don't you?"

Chapter 7

Sebastian stared into those fiery amber-brown eyes and realized his life had changed irrevocably. He was her slave. He dropped to his knees and gripped her cheeks with his rough palms. "Decent?" His laugh was almost maniacal. "It was the most indecent thing imaginable. You are filthy."

Her eyes clouded, suddenly uncertain, and she looked to be waiting for his verdict. Which was even more laughable, since—in his mind—she was already judge, jury, and executioner over his eternally shackled soul.

When he kissed her, he tasted the particular essence that was Anna, and then a hint of himself on her lips, and then the sweet blend of the two of them together. He wanted all of her, everywhere—with her tongue sliding against his, like now; with her fingers delving inside him, like before. He wanted her to be coursing through his blood.

It took a few beats before he realized she wasn't kissing him back. He forced himself to pull away, breathless.

"What is it, my sweet, wonderful Anna? Have I frightened you with my ardor?" He stroked her cheek with the pad of his thumb. "Because that seems impossible. You are fearless, are you not?"

"I am not fearless." She tried to look away, but he held her gaze.

"Well, then, whatever you are when you are swept away like you were just now, whatever that was, it is glorious and splendid and every spectacular word I can think of, and I am in awe."

She blushed, but he could tell it was pride at her burgeoning control over him, rather than embarrassment. She was pleased. With herself. With him. The idea slid through him like hot oil through his veins: he would do anything to please her.

"Now lean back, if you will, and let me taste you—" He tried to position her on the velvet sofa as he lowered himself to his knees and attempted to lift her skirts.

She resisted immediately. "Oh. That won't be necessary!" She wriggled away from him, her hands patting her disheveled hair and her back straightening as if she were a governess in the schoolroom. *Back to your studies, children.*

Sebastian laughed and then rested his palms on either side of her on the sofa. "Aren't you lovely when you're high-handed. Please, may I?"

"I didn't think most men enjoyed that sort of thing," she hedged.

Sebastian burst out laughing again. "Do you mistake me for *most men*?"

She smiled and put her palm to his cheek. "You are quite endearing, but really, you don't have to do that."

He turned and kissed her palm, letting his eyes drift shut as his lips made contact. When he opened his eyes and spoke, his voice was low. "I know I don't *have* to, darling. I *want* to. I'm desperate to please you."

She looked at him for a few moments, a mix of anxiety and calculation flashing across her face. He didn't care if she was cunning, as long as she let him devour her the way she had devoured him.

"What are you thinking?" he whispered. Her hand remained on his cheek. He stayed on his knees and tried to keep his hands still while he awaited her approval.

"I really shouldn't," she whispered in reply, but he saw her waver. "I mean, I don't think it appeals to me."

He had been reaching one hand slowly under her dress while she spoke. Now he looked at her with his best mischievous smile, and when his fingers touched the hot, wet mess between her legs, he said, "I think it appeals to you very much, my dear." He began to move his fingers slowly up and down her seam. Her head tilted back, and she draped her forearm over her eyes. "Very much."

She moaned, and her hips bucked to meet his hand.

"Please may I taste you?" he whispered even softer, in time with his stroking fingers.

"Oh dear God, forgive me. Yes."

He moved quickly, lest she change her mind. He spread her legs wide and had her splayed out on the velvet sofa in seconds as he pushed aside the layers of her gown.

"How lovely . . ." he said on a contented exhale as he kissed his way up her inner thigh. He was riled by the scent of her moist heat, too impatient to take the time to remove her underclothes. He found the slit in her linen and tore it wide. She gasped at the sound of ripping fabric. Then she began to murmur her encouragement—directions really. When his tongue lashed out and circled her clit, her hips bucked again and she nearly wailed, muffling the sound against her forearm.

"Oh, dear. You are good, Sebastian . . . so good."

His. This woman was his. Meant for him. For him to spend his life pleasing. Being good for her. The sound of her breathy approval sent his already fast-beating heart into a mad race.

He pushed her thighs even wider and spread her farther apart for his admiration and attention. He licked and taunted until she was panting hoarsely, ordering him to finish her off.

Right before she came—her left hand tugging on his hair ferociously, driving him hard against her—her cries had been reduced to torn pieces of language, her voice nothing less than the primal sound of pure desire.

She shoved his face away from her sensitized flesh and pulled him up the length of her body as she shuddered and quaked, her neck thrown back in satisfied abandon as she held him close. A flush of color suffused her chest and neck, her cheeks. How he could have ever mistaken her for a pale, wispy thing, he had no idea. She was hard steel and fire. Even the way she lounged beneath and alongside his body, as if he were there merely to cushion her. Which he supposed he was.

After she had calmed and he could feel her straightening, putting her metaphorical disguise back in place as she adjusted her skirts, he asked, "So . . . who is Pia?"

She looked confused, then pretended she hadn't heard or didn't know or wasn't going to answer. When he kept looking, waiting for a reply, she said, "An old friend."

"Do you love her?"

She didn't falter that time. She nodded once. "I do."

Sebastian pulled her closer against him and let her weep into his handkerchief.

Chapter 8

tupid, stupid woman! Anna must have cried out the only name she'd ever cried out in similar moments of self-forgetting and sensual oblivion. She wasn't even sure. Why had she ever agreed to let Sebastian pleasure her in that way? That was never part of any plan.

She had betrayed Pia unforgivably. Her mind was awash with guilt, a churning mess of missing Pia and wanting to rail at the injustice of it all—that something as seemingly simple as living a quiet life with the person she loved had forced her so far into this treachery. Still, even as she tasted the bitter guilt of having broken the single promise Pia had ever asked her to make, the residual pleasure of her climax confused her. Satisfaction and guilt. Indulgence and regret. She felt as if she were suffocating under the weight of it. Pia would despise her if she ever found out.

"Did I say her name?" Anna asked between gulps, once the racking tears had begun to subside.

Sebastian seemed almost amused, as if her torment were a mere trifle. "Yes. Quite lovely, really. Something for me to hope for one day."

"To hope for? Why?" Anna asked, wiping the damnable tears from her cheeks.

"Why, to hear my name on your lips with the same delirious abandon and satisfaction, of course."

"You're not angry?" She patted her face one last time with his handkerchief and then stared down at the beautiful needlework at the edge of the elegant linen, sewing with which she was so familiar. Hours and hours of her young life had been spent making perfect hems exactly like this one.

"Angry?" He pulled her chin up so she was forced to look in his eyes. "I meant what I said earlier, you beautiful girl. It wasn't only the physical acts . . ."

Her face flushed in brief embarrassment. Had she really done all those things to him—with such fervor—and let him do all those things to her in return? Pia often said Anna took on a feverish intensity when they were making love, almost out of her head.

He continued carefully. "I want to give myself to you, Anna. I want you."

She shivered at the seriousness of his tone. A lifetime of preparing to be subjected to men made it difficult to understand his words. When he said *I want you*, she heard *I want to own you*, as if he wanted to acquire her. Which could never happen, not if she were ever to be free of the shackles of all men. Without intending to, she stiffened in his arms. She was too confused. Everything was happening out of order. She needed to see Pia again. They needed to discuss their plans in more detail. She needed more time before she went to Madrid. These things were supposed to happen over time. She was supposed to become someone's mistress, nothing more. She felt the panic spread like a creeping mold in a damp cellar. Sebastian had the look of someone who wanted far more.

She spoke carefully, in an attempt to stem the slow, tormenting terror rising up from her gut. She had betrayed Pia. She had betrayed herself. "I know I was terribly wanton, but nothing can come of it—"

He pressed one finger against her lips, and it stilled her thoughts as well as her words. He set her slightly away from him so she was sitting on the couch. He knelt down in front of her, on one knee. She was appalled but did not have any idea how to stop what was clearly about to happen. If there were some way to claw herself out of her own skin, she would have tried it. Surely the man was not willing to offer anything more than an arrangement. *Which*, some part of her rational mind scrambled, *might be a workable solution*. Her thoughts scurried around like little mice, frantic. *Pia, what am I to do?*

He took her hand in his.

Surely . . . not.

"No," she whispered, covering her mouth with the handkerchief clenched in her free hand and widening her eyes in anticipation.

"My dearest Anna, will you do me the great honor of becoming my wife?"

"Your *wife*?" she blurted. Even to her own ears she sounded shrill and shrewish.

His face softened. "Yes, Anna. *My wife.* Or would you rather be my mistress?" His smile made it perfectly clear he considered that last bit an absurdity, as if *any* woman in all of Europe—or in all the world, for that matter—would rather be Sebastian de Montizon's mistress instead of his lawfully wedded wife with all the wealth and prestige the title conferred.

Her heart pounded. *Think, think, think.* "I need to think. It's all so . . . unexpected."

"Really? Did you not expect to marry *ever*? Or did you not expect to marry *me*?"

"We've only just met. We're practically strangers. We *are* strangers."

Sebastian stood up from his kneeling position and pulled at the pristine white edge of his shirt cuff, where it peeked out from his expensive green coat. "Really, Anna," he practically clucked. He looked down at her, letting his eyes slide over the length of her body, then his tongue swept across his upper lip in greedy memory. "I can still taste you. We are far from strangers. In fact, I would venture to say we are intimately acquainted."

She jumped up from her inferior position on the couch and put her hands on her hips. She needed to collect herself. He kept smiling down at her. *Why was he so damned tall?* She spied a footrest near where he was standing and stepped onto it. Now they were at eye level, which only seemed to amuse Sebastian further. His smile widened as he rested one elbow on the mantelpiece with casual confidence.

Anna almost growled at his arrogance. "Stop looking at me like that."

"Like what? Like I adore you? I don't think I'll ever be able to wipe that expression from my face. And why should I?"

"Oh! You are so entirely accustomed to getting your own way, aren't you?"

"Hmm. An attribute we have in common, perhaps?"

She fisted her hands at her waist.

"Are you going to take a swing at me for proposing matrimony?" he asked, that twinkle in his eye letting her know he wouldn't be entirely opposed to the idea.

"I should, you know. You're so impertinent. You deserve a good spanking, is what you deserve."

His nostrils flared, and his eyes widened. "You cannot imagine how the thought delights me."

"Sebastian!" She tried to sound stern, but his fervor was contagious and her exasperation was tinged with humor.

"Yes?" He was soft again, reaching out to touch a piece of the lacy fabric near her wrist.

Anna sighed. He was entirely too adorable. Emboldened by her silence, he started tracing his finger along the sensitive skin of her wrist. If he was even half as smitten as he claimed to be, maybe she could negotiate after all. She had to think clearly. She had to think of Pia.

"What do I stand to gain from this proposal?" she asked, as if she were haggling with the milliner in Burgos.

He reared back his head and laughed in that all-encompassing way of his. "You are spectacular, you know that? Other than my splendid self, of course, there will be travels and adventures and riches beyond your imagining."

"Be careful what you promise," she warned. "I suspect there's not much beyond my imagining."

He smiled and held her hand tighter. "I will soon be a very wealthy man—I don't mean it in a boastful or crass way. I only say it to let you know that whatever you wish for will be within my grasp to provide."

She contemplated his words in all their meaning. "But, sweet Sebastian, what if I wish for freedom?"

"Then you shall have it," he answered without hesitation. "As my wife, you may enjoy any liberty you wish."

She lowered her eyes and stared at their joined hands. "And what if I wish for Pia?"

He leaned down with a gallant flourish to kiss the back of her hand, then stood up tall and proud. "If that is the case—"

Chapter 9

efore Sebastian had a chance to finish, the door to the library swung open under the weight of two entwined lovers. Anna nearly burst out laughing when the newlyweds tumbled into the room and the door slammed shut behind them.

"At last—" Javi gasped before covering Isabella's mouth with his own. She caught sight of Anna and Sebastian across the room and groaned, trying to push him away, but he pulled her harder against him, apparently mistaking her sounds of resistance for an attempt to stoke his passion.

"Javi!" She finally wrenched herself away and slapped him across the face, presumably to douse his enthusiasm.

His eyes gleamed dark and seductive at the provocation. "Ah, Isabella—" He put his hand on his cheek as if he wanted to relive the sting of her flesh against his. "My fiery wife, you will be punished for that—"

She fisted her hands on her hips. "Javi, we are not alone!"

He turned quickly, letting his hand drop from his face. "Sebastian. What the hell are you doing in here?"

Anna admired the defiant set of Sebastian's shoulders.

"I am in the midst of proposing marriage to Anna Redondo, if you must know." He stepped aside to reveal her—standing on the silly step stool next to the fireplace where she had been partially concealed behind his broad back.

Anna stepped down and tried to repress a sigh at the incoming explosion that was Isabella. Her friend had grabbed bunches of her white lace wedding gown and was running across the library. She halted at the turn of the sofa to stare at Anna with a theatrical gasp.

"Anna! What in the world— Where is Sister Elvira? Why are you unchaperoned? How long have you known Sebastian? Why did you not tell me of your affection?" Anna watched as Isabella turned her irritated confusion on Sebastian, stomping one foot for effect. "What have you done to her? She looks like she's been crying!" Dramatically dropping the fabric of her gown, Isabella grabbed Anna's hands in hers. "Are you unwell? Did he hurt you?"

Anna's face felt hot and mottled. She probably looked a fright. How to answer such a question . . . Had he raised her to the heights of physical pleasure? Had he made a mockery of her promises to Pia? And then, perhaps, offered her a chance at a new and beautiful future? Yes. And yes. And yes.

But she could not get any words out. He had never—he would never—*hurt* her.

"Anna!" Isabella pulled her into a protective one-armed hug and turned to glare at Sebastian, then barked, "How could you? I thought you were a gentleman!"

Sebastian looked affronted. Justifiably so. She tried to wrest herself away from the temporary comfort of her friend's embrace, but Isabella only tightened her grip.

"I?" he cried, pointing at his chest. "I have offered for her! I am Sebastian de Montizon and she is a convent girl of questionable parentage—"

"How dare you!" Isabella finally released Anna and took a step closer to Sebastian, her rigid posture mimicking his. She pulled her fist back to take a swing at him, but Javi's strong fingers caught her wrist an instant before she made contact.

Javi had kept quiet until now—always stealthy whether he was skulking around the forest or reposing in a ducal library. Perhaps unwisely, he tried to intercede. "Darling . . ."

Isabella wrenched her hand from his. "Don't call me *darling*! Call him out! He has insulted my dear friend."

Javi started laughing. "He has offered to *marry* her, my love. How can I possibly call him out for doing what is right and honorable?"

"Honorable? Look at her." Isabella pointed at Anna as if she were something battered and worn that had been tossed onto the docks in Aveiro. "She has obviously been . . . taken advantage of."

Javi's face stormed. "Sebastian . . . did you—"

Now it was Sebastian's turn to become infuriated. "Javi. How dare you?" He pointed in Anna's direction. "She—"

Anna finally spoke up, resting one hand on Sebastian's forearm to stay him. "Please, all of you." She gave Isabella an exasperated look. "Do stop speaking about me as if I am a parcel."

The other three stood still and said nothing.

"Very well," Anna said on a sigh. It wasn't how she had planned it, but it certainly wasn't the worst possible outcome. Perhaps Sebastian would let her visit Pia occasionally. Perhaps in time, something could be arranged. *Perhaps.* It was a thin hope, but it was all Anna had.

Sebastian smiled as if he were reading her thoughts. He wanted to please her, or so he'd said. She looked at him a moment longer, then nodded. "I accept."

Sebastian pulled her into a gleeful embrace, lifting her small frame off the ground and twirling her once around before setting her back in place. Javi and Isabella wore nearly identical expressions of complete shock.

Isabella spoke first. "You? Anna— You what?"

Anna looked away from Sebastian and those victorious, possessive eyes of his. His happiness was so exuberant as to be almost terrifying. "I accepted his offer."

"But," Isabella said, "it's only Javi and myself. No one need know of your indiscretion if you do not wish it."

Sebastian growled at the implication.

Isabella growled in return. "What? You cannot simply marry her because you've . . ." Her voice trailed off.

He smirked and put his arm around Anna's small waist, tucking her closer into him. "Because I've *what*, Isabella?" he challenged. "I'm sure you're not about to imply anything improper about my fiancée, otherwise I'd have to call *you* out."

Javi was obviously torn between years of loyalty to his best friend and his newfound, but no less compelling, loyalty to his wife. He reached his arm around Isabella's waist. Anna suspected he was not sure what else to do.

"Y-y-you've . . ." Isabella stammered, then furrowed her brows and turned her gaze to Anna. She lowered her voice, and Anna recognized the familiar inner battle of Isabella attempting to master her temper. "Are you sure, Anna? Is this truly what you want?"

Anna stood up straighter and realized this part, this new role, had to begin now. She pulled her shoulders back and leaned more easily into Sebastian. She looked up at him one last time. He would never hurt her, not intentionally. He was playful and kind. She would be the wife of an aristocrat, maybe one day able to wield enough power to reclaim the woman she loved. She smiled at the idea, and he smiled back, as if reading the direction of her thought and not finding it appalling.

Sebastian had a way about him, a military efficiency beneath his amusement that led Anna to hope he, if anyone, could make that happen. Somehow.

She turned back to Isabella. "Yes. This is what I want."

Isabella still was not convinced. She opened her mouth, but her husband interrupted before she could elaborate on her displeasure.

"There. Everyone is happy." Javi spoke quickly, as if he'd handily repaired a wheel on a carriage and now they would all make it to the ball in a timely fashion.

Isabella stared at Anna, silently willing her to say more. When Anna did not, Isabella turned on her husband, opening her mouth again, obviously on the verge of saying something pointed and rude. Before she said a word, however, she must have caught the look of feral delight in Javi's eyes.

"Think before you speak, my darling wife."

Anna watched as some powerful, unspoken negotiation passed between them. Isabella looked as if she wanted to lose her temper further, maybe even to vex her husband on purpose, but then her face changed. The heady desire that passed between bride and groom permeated the huge room. Javi smiled, almost willing her to defy him.

In a moment of near magic, Isabella transformed her entire being from a bundle of petulance to noble grace. She lowered herself into a delicate curtsey. "My lord." She bowed her head without a hint of irony and stayed perfectly still in that lowered position. Javi trailed one finger along her pale, elegant neck, and she shivered visibly at the light touch.

When he looked up to see Sebastian and Anna, Javi was already beginning to remove one of his leather gloves. "Please leave us," he said, dismissing them with a brief nod.

Chapter 10

ebastian laughed, and Anna gasped. He pulled her along with him as they headed out of the library. Anna kept glancing over her shoulder as they crossed the large room. She was enthralled by Isabella in that completely beatific pose, holding her head at that exquisitely submissive angle while Javi stalked around her, removing his other glove, then trailing the soft leather along Isabella's neck and shoulders.

"Enough gawking for now, my dear." Sebastian's amused voice pulled her back from that strangely alluring tableau. He closed the door and surprised her by pulling her into a warm embrace, his back against the stone wall and her body flush up against his front. "Do you want to be the one on your knees or the one with the glove?" he asked, his breath hot and his voice eager between kisses.

"The glove . . ." Her words escaped on a moan that betrayed the truth of them.

He laughed low and raw against her neck, kissing her and licking her. "I suspected as much. How delightfully convenient . . ."

Anna inhaled sharply, unable to believe his words. "You . . . you would kneel for me . . . like that?"

"Oh, my dear. I believe kneeling is the veriest start of what I will do to please you."

Her mind flooded with images: Sebastian perfectly still and beautiful for her, like Isabella had been for Javi, like Pia had been for Anna in the past. So willing, so pliant, so receptive . . . Oh, the possibilities. Anna's face clouded in guilt when she thought of Pia in those same positions, so eager and loving. Could Anna be so changeable, so easily distracted from the one person who had brought her the only joy she'd ever known?

"What is it, love?" Sebastian stared into her eyes. "Is it your lover? Do you miss Pia?"

She nodded but firmed her lips. "I will try to learn to forget her. I have accepted your offer. There is nothing more to be done."

He narrowed his eyes, and her heart began to speed up. "There is always more to be done, my love."

"What can possibly be done? Pia has no connections, no family to speak of. How will she ever escape the convent now if I should abandon her?"

"Why would you abandon her?"

"Why? What? Because I have agreed to marry you—" Anna was becoming frantic with a mix of hope and fear.

"Shhh," he soothed. "We three shall live together, of course." His hands were roving across her ribs and waist, touching her everywhere. "With Pia as your companion—*our* companion, if I'm to be truly blessed—but nothing untoward as far as the outside world is concerned. I shall write a letter to the abbess right after supper to let her know of our betrothal and our eager wish to have Pia as a member of our household. Nothing to it."

Anna's mind had been so knotted for so long. Convoluted plans and machinations were the only remedies at her disposal. She wanted to rail against the injustice of a society that kept her and Pia locked behind walls while this man could move human beings like chess pieces with the flick of his quill.

But she would take. And take some more. Perhaps that made her complicit in her own oppression, but she was no fool. This man was giving her his power, asking her to take it. *Kneeling is the veriest start . . .*

Her thoughts crystallized as he found her wet heat again. He'd slipped his ungloved hand under her dress while she'd been thinking. "We are in the hall, my lord . . ." Her breath was short.

"Are we? I hadn't noticed."

"Yes, write the letter, Sebastian. You will make me a very happy woman." She rested her palm over his heart and felt it accelerate at her praise. "Very happy," she repeated in a lower tone of voice.

"Let me pleasure you once again before we have to sit through that interminable wedding supper. Please." The combination of his supplicating voice and the not-so-distant murmur of other guests who could happen upon them at any moment whipped her into a new froth of desire. "You like that we are risking discovery, don't you?" he whispered, teasing her silky flesh with his strong fingers.

She bit his earlobe, hard, in reply, reveling in his answering moan of pain-pleasure. "Let's see which one of us enjoys the risk more," she challenged. "Open your trousers and let me hold your cock while you pleasure me with your hand."

And, oh, how he wanted to be told to do it. His breathless hesitation was glorious. She licked his earlobe where she'd bitten him. "Now."

He let out a stifled cry of submission and quickly unbuttoned the placket of his trousers. She adjusted her skirts so he was mostly concealed if anyone passed by the other end of the long hall. And then his greedy mouth was on hers, his fingers finding her again through the layers of fabric, her hand wrapped tight around his hard length as she pumped him until he begged for release.

"No," she growled, wanting to drag out his pleasure until he was beyond desperation.

He turned his hand inside her and pumped into her with the same rhythm she was using on him. She cried out, the sound muffled by his kiss, and then felt the slick warmth of his release coat her hand a few seconds later.

He let his hand rest amid the heat and pressure of the layers of fabric, as he recovered from a white-hot grip of desire unlike any he'd ever imagined. When he'd felt her shudder and pulse against his fingers, his cock had exploded in an answering cry. He moaned against her mouth, drawing out every last remnant of her pleasure with long strokes of his fingers. He'd always loved the taste and smell of women, but this woman was something else entirely. After one final kiss of appreciation against her swollen lips, he pulled his hand out from under her skirts. He used the wall like the back of a chair and squatted to adjust his trousers and rebutton himself. When he finished, he rested his forearms against his bent knees and tried to catch his breath.

"Come here, my sweet." Her voice was so gentle and loving, so different from the commanding growl he'd responded to moments before. He loved them both.

He rose up to his full height.

"Clean me," she whispered. She held out the delicate hand she had used to grip his cock, and he stared at the glistening evidence of his release.

"What would you have me do?" His voice cracked, unable to conceal his interest.

"Taste yourself on me." She put her fingers into his mouth, and he was lost to the sensation of it, his eyes drifting closed as he entered that dream state she seemed to be able to hurl him into whenever it pleased her. "I think we shall get along admirably, don't you?"

He sucked her slowly, licking between her fingers, along her palm, and then around each of the sensitive tips. He finished with a hot kiss into her palm. "Yes," he finally answered. "I believe we shall get along splendidly. Especially once I contact the convent, and the three of us are joined."

She dove at him then, devouring his mouth with kisses of gratitude and renewed pleasure. "Three," she whispered between kisses. "Think of it."

"Believe me," he said on a low laugh. "I have."

As she kissed him more deeply, he sensed that she was floating back into the current of sensual desire, tasting the two of them on his lips. "Oh my, you are delicious," she said, her voice full of wonder.

He laughed at the back of his throat. "Perhaps you think *yourself* delicious."

"No," she whispered, "I think you and I mixed together . . . we are something else entirely . . . delicious . . ."

Chapter 11

Many long hours later, Sebastian got Anna almost to himself in a far corner of the bustling postprandial drawing room. He let her know that he'd sent a courier with letters to his parents in Madrid and to the abbess of the convent in Burgos, telling them of his intention to marry her. He'd also told the abbess that his fiancée's dear friend Pia was needed in their entourage and that they would arrive four weeks hence to retrieve her.

"Oh, I wish I could've written a short postscript to Pia."

"I'm sorry I didn't think of it."

Anna smiled at his contrition, and it warmed his blood. "It's probably best that I stay silent," she added after a few seconds, looking out across the crowded room, sparkling with candlelight and bejeweled aristocrats.

"Why is that, darling?" Already he longed to touch her whenever they spoke.

She must have sensed it. Anna reached out and skimmed a finger near his waist, knowing he was standing at an angle that prevented any of the people in the room from seeing the small contact. He felt the slight touch reverberate through every muscle in his body.

She smiled at his reaction, then withdrew her hand and continued. "I probably would have been overly effusive in my correspondence. I'm fairly certain the abbess was beginning to suspect something *untoward* had developed between the two of us. If I'd given the cruel woman any reason to suspect more, I know she would do everything in her power to prevent our happiness."

"I believe my request shall not be denied."

Anna raised an eyebrow in inquiry.

"I mentioned how the extent of my gratitude at having secured the affections of my future wife would only be exceeded by my generosity to the convent upon my arrival to retrieve her dear companion."

Anna's smile was complicit. "You are a naughty one, aren't you? Do you always get what you want?"

He shrugged, the thrill of pleasing her simmering to the surface once again. "If it means fulfilling your desires, then yes. I shan't stop at anything."

She leaned in slightly and whispered, "You will be rewarded handsomely, Sebastian."

He shivered and stood up taller, regaining his composure as an elderly aristocrat from Madrid passed nearby.

"Sebastian." The man was a friend of his father's and gave Sebastian a haughty look.

"Sir," Sebastian replied, acknowledging him with a formal nod. "Please allow me to present my fiancée, Anna Redondo. Anna, this is the Conde de Frigiliana."

She curtseyed, and the man bowed, giving her a scrutinizing appraisal, and went on his way.

"Bastard." Sebastian muttered under his breath, then smiled back at Anna and continued quietly, "You'll have to pardon my disdain for the so-called leaders who are blindly giving Spain to the enemy."

"I have heard tell of the arrival of Napoleon's brother in May, but I am far from informed when it comes to political intrigue," she said. "It sounds interesting. I hope you will enlighten me."

He narrowed his eyes. "It sounds interesting to you?"

"Of course it does." She looked affronted. "Do you think I enjoy being a twig on the river of civilization merely because I was born a girl?"

He shook his head slowly. "You could never be a twig on any river, dear Anna."

She still looked ruffled.

"And to be clear, yes, I will look forward to enlightening you when it comes to the events that are shaping our government and our world." His eyes narrowed again. "In fact, I believe you and Pia will be an integral part of what I hope to achieve in London on an upcoming trip Javi has asked me to take."

"How wonderful!" Anna exclaimed. "I have always wanted to see that city, to go to the theater, and meet some of the writers and philosophers there."

"Have you now?"

"Yes, very much. But as you must know by now, I'm not as accustomed to getting what I want as you are."

"I find that hard to believe."

"Well, in the wider world, I suppose"—she smiled up at him—"I have not as much experience exerting my will."

"We must remedy that as soon and as often as possible," he said with an answering smile. After they spoke to another passing wedding guest, Sebastian asked her, "Is there anyone else to whom I should speak about my proposal?" Once everyone was well out of earshot, he continued, "Have you no relative or guardian to whom I should apply?"

Anna shook her head. "No one . . . or at least no one who cares about my future."

"Who is your father, Anna? Have you no idea?"

Anna looked down at the tips of the satin slippers Isabella had lent her for the day. "I knew I would have to tell you of my sordid past eventually, but I had not anticipated doing so this soon."

He waited for her to go on.

Taking a deep breath, she looked up into Sebastian's eyes and spoke warily. "My mother was married to the Conde de Floridablanca when she had me. You probably know him as José Moñino y Redondo. He was much older than she."

Sebastian nodded in recognition of the old and powerful family name from decades past.

"My mother . . . loved another man. After she became pregnant with his child, she hoped she could pass me off as the legitimate heir of her elderly husband. But when I was born with the blonde hair and telling mark of the English diplomat who had been billeted in my father's *castillo* in 1788 . . ." Her voice faded as she fingered the slightly raised patch of dark-brown skin at the base of her neck.

Sebastian wanted desperately to lean in and kiss the delicate birthmark. Apparently sensing his desire, Anna shivered.

"I love it," he whispered. "It is a mark of passion that refuses to be denied."

He looked into her eyes, and he felt a new heat, a new connection building between them. Not only the warmth of their young bodies craving each other, but the way their minds worked.

"You are nothing like the cruel, domineering men the nuns always describe." Her face softened. "So tender and eager to please." Her praise warmed him like a caress. "You are a very good man, Sebastian. A very unusual one, I think."

He hummed his gratitude and leaned more heavily against the column at his side. Not being able to touch her was proving difficult.

"Do you want to touch me very badly, Sebastian? Even here in front of all of these prying noblemen?" Of course she had noticed he was struggling, and the wicked woman was enjoying it. The realization that she could taunt him here in a crowded room as easily as she could toy with him in an empty library or a deserted hallway brought a mischievous smile to her face. "Do you want your lips on me again, you greedy boy?" Her voice was soft, her expression light and cheerful. If anyone glimpsed them talking, it would appear they were discussing something of little importance, the violinist or the *membrillo* that had been served after supper.

She rubbed the tip of her finger along her lower lip, and he practically groaned. She glanced down at his firming cock. "That's it, my sweet Sebastian. So responsive. So giving." She let her hand slip away from her lips and stared into his eyes.

"I am yours, Anna," he said quietly. "In every possible way a man can offer himself to a woman, I offer myself to you. I submit my body into your keeping."

"I will treasure the gift of your submission, Sebastian." She was no longer toying with him. "Of course, I will honor and obey you as society expects; in the eyes of the world you will always be my lord. But . . ." He moaned, and a shiver of delight passed through him. "But, in the bedroom . . ." Her words caused him to stop breathing. "But in the bedroom, *you* shall honor and obey *me* . . . as we both know you crave it." She looked away and smiled innocently at an elderly woman who passed nearby.

"I do . . . I do crave it . . ." Sebastian whispered hoarsely.

"In the privacy of our own world"—she said without turning toward him—"there is so much we can explore together . . . we three . . . inextricably bound."

"Anna . . ." His throat constricted with emotion.

"I know, Sebastian. It will be beautiful."

He closed his eyes and tapped the side of his head against the stone column until the physical pain brought him back from the brink of spending himself in the middle of the crowded drawing room.

Chapter 12

ia started pacing as soon as the abbess left the small chamber. Her sharp mind dulled with the news she had been given. *A lady's maid? To Anna?* Was hers to be a lifetime of bitter torment, watching her lover be controlled and dominated by such a man as the infamous Sebastian de Montizon? Or worse, what if Anna actually loved him?

Either way, Pia had been given word that her life was to become a circle of hell. She forced a tight fist into her mouth to stifle her anguished cry.

At first, she'd been overwhelmed with joy when the abbess gave her the news that Anna was coming to retrieve her. To see Anna! Oh, how her heart sang at the prospect! To kiss that place at the back of her neck where the palest wisps of blonde hair pointed to the straight perfection of her spine. To feel Anna's nearly careless petting and touching while Pia curled at the foot of Anna's bed or rested her head in Anna's lap.

Then tears of misery threatened when the abbess elaborated, "She *and her husband* will arrive in a few weeks to collect you." To never have those things again would have been torture enough, but to live in the constant presence of the man who was receiving that touch in her stead? To know *he* was receiving those greedy kisses? She wasn't sure she could bear it.

Patrizia Velasquez Carvajal was strong in every way imaginable. She was tall and formidable, with hard muscles along her thighs and hips and shoulders; she was a respected member of her small community; she was a capable person when it came to organizing projects or navigating the political nuances of convent life. But she wasn't strong when it came to Anna. The mere thought of Anna Redondo turned Pia Carvajal into a weak, useless thing.

She thought of how Anna had made her—*made her! Ha! Made her* want to, *more like*—unwind the long strip of linen that she used to bind her breasts, and how the cool autumn air had trailed against her nipples, and how the pressure of Anna's appreciative eyes on her tender flesh had made her breasts feel heavy and full, desperate for more. Always desperate for more of Anna's gaze. Anna's touch.

And then how Anna had approached her, making the anticipation crackle between them even more keenly. And then when Anna's mouth had been on her, sucking and teasing, biting and punishing, until Pia had felt wave after wave of crashing pleasure break apart inside her.

Even now she could feel an approaching climax at the recollection—without even a touch between her legs, without anything but the memory of that greedy mouth, with nothing but the faintest reminiscence of Anna's desire and her hoarse command, "Come for me."

All those blessed memories now only brought more tears. More stifled groans of misery.

Anna probably kissed that beast of a man with that beautiful mouth of hers. She probably submitted to him, losing the spark and honor that made her who she was. The force of steel that resided in that deceptively small body had probably been bent to his will. The greatness that was Anna's power had probably been destroyed or subsumed by an arrogant prick.

Pia wiped her eyes and patted her face dry with her apron. In several weeks she would see for herself. That's when the *newlyweds* were due to pick up their *lady's maid*. Pia stood up straighter, despising everything those words implied.

She would see Anna one last time. She would see that she was safe, at least. She would let herself be taken out of the convent, out of Spain. She would let herself be taken to London.

And then Pia would run.

Chapter 13

For the few weeks before they were due in Madrid, Anna and Sebastian rusticated in Feria with Javi and Isabella. Banns were posted in the capital, and Sebastian's parents were delighted their son had finally agreed to marry a virginal Spanish miss.

During that idyllic time, Sebastian and Javi spent many hours in the corral, while Isabella and Anna strolled with their parasols beneath the warm sun and pretended to admire their horsemanship. While both men were excellent equestrians, Anna and Isabella were far more preoccupied with the fit of male trousers and the turn of muscled hips.

For the first time in her life, Anna felt like she could breathe without the pressing need to worry about her future or calculate her prospects. The summer dresses that Isabella had given her felt less confining, the jaunty straw hats more playful than the rigid ones she'd been forced to wear in Burgos. Anna realized she had never been at leisure, and she relished every second now. She listened to the wind as it wound its way through the cork oak forest at night. She read volume after volume from Isabella's library. She dreamt of Pia. And, as the days passed, she dreamt of Sebastian.

On this particular afternoon, ten days after the wedding, Anna and Isabella were once again watching the men in the riding ring (and pretending to see their equestrian skills). The crunch of the gravel path beneath their feet offset the rhythm of the trotting horses.

"Sebastian is quite a good rider," Isabella conceded, squinting her eyes and pausing to lean against the white wall of the enclosure. Since she was apparently unable to see the radiance of any male but her new husband, everything Isabella said about Sebastian sounded reluctant.

Anna nodded her head in agreement. "He is."

"Have you really fallen in love with him?" Isabella asked, turning her attention away from the prancing Arabians—and their handsome riders—to focus on Anna.

Sebastian and Anna had not been alone since their time in the library. Ironically, the public announcement of their future matrimony had put a complete halt to any private assignations until the blessed event came to pass. The elderly nun with whom she'd traveled had recovered fully from her weariness, and since the day her betrothal was announced, Anna had either been with Isabella or with the old shrew of a chaperone nearly attached to her elbow.

As a result, the physical heat and wonder of Sebastian's body had gradually been replaced by something more subtle, and perhaps more dangerous. Anna furrowed her brow at the realization. "I don't know much of love, really. I believe he will be a good husband, and that is more than I ever dared hope for."

"Why have you always tempered your dreams so?"

"What a strange thing to say, Isabella."

"Don't evade."

"Very well. I was not, as you say, tempering my dreams. You and I have had these differences for the many years of our friendship. I was not born to this way of life." She looked toward the splendid *alcázar*, with its extensive manicured gardens and buzzing apiary in the distance. "Even the bees enjoy luxurious accommodations here."

"You always say that this world is foreign to you," Isabella replied impatiently, "but deep down, your blood is as blue as mine."

"You are a terrible snob, Isabella." When she reddened at the small insult, Anna quickly added, "I didn't mean it as a cut."

Isabella pursed her lips.

"Oh, well, perhaps I did," Anna admitted. "A bit. But I only meant that your view of the world is so fixed. How could it be any other way? Your path has been set since you were born in that palace. There was no point in my dreaming of this sort of life."

"There is always a point in dreaming." Isabella spoke softly, looking back to admire her magnificent husband. "What if I had never pursued my dream of escape? I would have never met Javi."

Anna considered her logic. "Perhaps I will grow to love Sebastian the way you love Javi. You did not love him right away, did you?"

Isabella blushed. "No. In fact, I found him rather impossible. It would have made much more sense for me to fall in love with someone more appropriate like . . . well, like Sebastian."

Anna was unable to repress a small chuckle at how *inappropriate* Sebastian could be.

Isabella smiled in return. "What is funny?"

"Nothing," Anna said. "Pray continue. Why would Sebastian have been a more appropriate match?"

"Because he is from a good family, obviously, and he's so much more *amenable* than Javi, and quite handsome as well, don't you think?" Isabella asked.

"I suppose . . ." Anna felt the skin at the back of her neck tingle when she thought of Sebastian's *amenability*. He happened to turn his horse and smile at her at just that moment; Anna marveled at how he was so open, so unafraid of showing his affection. The horse pulled in the other direction and the connection was lost.

"See? Even that!" Isabella chuckled. "He is certainly not the type of man one considers *comme ci, comme ça*. Sebastian is unquestionably handsome, yet you remain ambivalent. So. Are you still in love with Pia?"

Anna gasped, and a rush of hot embarrassment crept up her neck. "Isabella!" She had never suspected Isabella knew her secret, and she certainly didn't think she would treat it so lightly if she ever found out.

"What? You thought I didn't know?" She looked hard into Anna's eyes. "How stupid you must think me." Isabella looked back at the ring as the two men went galloping past. Isabella gave them a smile and a small wave. "Wave, Anna," she muttered between her teeth without letting her smile slip. Anna did as she was bid—waving briefly then returning her grip to the bamboo handle of her parasol—and hoped the interrogation about her life with Pia would be lost on the breeze along with the dust that the horses had kicked up.

She should have known better.

After the two caballeros had finished showing off, one of the grooms brought out another pair of quarter horses in need of exercise. They were skittish and excitable. Anna watched quietly as Sebastian dismounted and traded the reins of the horse he'd been riding for the more frantic of the two. Isabella was right after all: he was powerfully handsome. He rubbed his big, strong hand against the horse's satiny chestnut coat, following the contours of the quivering muscles along the beast's neck. The memory of that strong hand making its way up her inner thigh had Anna biting her lip in confusion. Her body had responded with thrilling ease to Sebastian's touch—even now, the mere sight of him across the corral had her shifting from one foot to another in agitation—but her feelings for Pia were so much more.

"I'll take your silence as a yes, then," Isabella said. "You are still attached to Pia in your heart."

"It's complicated. I never dreamt—"

Isabella's bark of a laugh startled the two new horses. She raised her hand and called her apology to Javi and Sebastian for the disruption. Without turning back to face Anna, she continued speaking. "That's precisely what I was saying. I never meant that you should dream of, oh, I don't know, impossibilities." She paused to collect her thoughts then tilted her head to look at Anna directly. "But there's nothing wrong with dreaming that certain things are indeed *possible*. The world is ours, don't you see? Whether princess or peasant, it is a moment in history when we may reach—" Isabella stopped suddenly. "I'm sorry. I become as excited as those horses when I think about all the possibilities. And Javi does not exclude me. That is the wonder of it all. We talk about everything and dream together. Of how the world is changing. Of grand political movements." Her voice went a bit lower. "And of how best to show our love for one another."

Anna nodded. "It is a lovely marriage you have."

Isabella stomped her booted foot. "That is not at all what I was driving at and you know it. Do you love him? Or are you still in love with Pia? At least be honest with yourself—even if you are not inclined to be honest with me."

"Oh, Bell." The warm summer air licked at Anna's bare shoulders, reminding her of a lover's touch. She wasn't sure she knew the truth of her own feelings. "I honestly don't know. I do love Pia. But I don't need to choose—"

"What?" Isabella screeched.

"Sebastian is willing to give me—"

Isabella's head spun so quickly her parasol whipped around, and she startled the horses again. "Sorry! Sorry!" she called to Javi and Sebastian.

Javi winked at them and called to his wife in a low drawl, "Perhaps you should take your important plotting and wild gesturing into the gardens, my love."

"Very well, my lord," she replied with mock obedience, then slipped her arm through Anna's and led her toward the extensive gardens on the far side of the castle.

They strolled in silence for many minutes, and Anna dreaded she was going to have to endure some sort of examination as a result of admitting the nature of her arrangement with Sebastian and Pia.

When they were deep into the gardens, behind a tall trellis of climbing roses, Anna let herself relax and be lulled into believing they were taking a quiet stroll, free of perceptive best friends and their pesky inquisitions.

Alas.

Isabella turned on her heel, retracted her parasol with a quick *click*, and speared the tip into the ground. "Anna!"

"What?"

"I can't believe I thought *you* were the one who was being taken advantage of in the library on my wedding day! Poor Sebastian."

"What do you mean by 'Poor Sebastian'?"

"I mean, *you* are using *him*."

Anna stood her ground and met Isabella head-on. "Are we going to be that honest? Truly?"

"Why not?" Isabella challenged.

"Very well then. Are you not *using* Javi? Did your marriage not allow you to return to your father's good graces? Do you not manipulate him in your way? Are not *all* marriages a mutual manipulation?"

They kept facing each other. Isabella tilted her head in thought as she twisted her parasol into the ground. "I see what you are saying . . ."

"But?"

"But I love Javi, dash it all, and he loves me."

"What difference does love make?" Anna asked, irritation trimming her words.

Isabella let her parasol drop abruptly and grabbed Anna's upper arm. "Love makes all the difference in the world!"

The words slammed through her. She knew they were true, but she was so confused. Anna knew she loved Pia, but was it so wrong to merely *like* Sebastian for now? She had never lied to him about her feelings, after all; she had never misled him with promises of anything more.

"Something done with love, even something cruel, can be so beautiful," Isabella continued. "I know you believe that. I saw how you were with Pia."

Once again, Isabella's words cut Anna to the quick and brought back a flood of memories—of Pia in her arms, panting and satisfied from the cruel, beautiful love Anna could bestow upon her. She nearly wept. "Were we so obvious?"

"Stop it, Anna. No one knew. I knew because I know *you*. I saw the subtle differences when you two were next to each other at meals or during prayers. You were softer somehow. That is what I mean. If you have no intention of *ever* giving that to Sebastian, why would you marry him?"

Anna looked away from her friend's stern face but didn't bother wiping at her own slow, hot tears. They burned like a fiery penance. "I am not a good person."

"Of course you are!" Isabella reached out and wiped Anna's tears away. "That's what I am attempting to convey, you stubborn girl. At least give yourself *permission* to love him, to learn to love him."

Anna huffed out a low laugh. "It's not at all what I had *planned*."

Isabella's laughter rang through the gardens. "Ah! The truth comes out. I call them dreams; you call them plans. Much the same, no?" Isabella closed the distance between them. "Please promise me that you will be open to the possibility of loving him?"

Anna was overcome. Making this particular promise was likely more important than her upcoming wedding vows. Allowing for the possibility—that she could one day love Sebastian—was allowing for so much. It meant that she believed she actually *deserved* to love him, and even more disarming, that she deserved to be loved in return. She took a breath, but it couldn't quite fill her lungs around the enormity of what was truly her first leap of faith. "Fine. I promise."

Isabella nodded her approval and bent to retrieve her parasol.

"Satisfied?" Anna quipped, trying to lighten the mood.

"No," Isabella replied quickly. "There's still the other matter."

Anna could tell Isabella was back to her mischievous self as they resumed strolling around the gardens. "Which other matter might that be?"

"So tell me."

"Tell you what?"

"Tell me . . . how in the world you got Sebastian to agree to letting you keep your relationship with Pia."

"Isabella!"

"What? You don't think I've asked Javi?" Isabella smiled.

"No!"

"Well, I did. I thought it might be fun, for variety's sake, mind you. Nothing serious, of course!"

Anna nodded slowly, knowing perfectly well what the possessive Javi's response to that must have been, but she played along. "And?"

"Never! He said he would never let another person in our bed. Man or woman. He was furious I'd suggested it." She winked. "As wicked as he is in other ways, I thought he'd see it as a bit of lark." Isabella shrugged.

"And then that was the end of it?"

"Hardly. He punished me for days for even broaching the subject." Anna was momentarily concerned until Isabella smiled again. "So we were both happy."

Anna laughed.

"So?" Isabella prompted again. "Share and share alike. How did you get Sebastian to agree to it?"

Anna smiled at all the brutal ways she knew she could get Sebastian to agree to anything she wished but said lightly, "I think Sebastian is quite looking forward to the possibilities."

"Oh dear." Isabella kicked a pebble and had a cross look of disappointment on her brow.

"What is it? Surely I cannot have shocked you."

"No, of course not. Now I shall be jealous."

Chapter 14

hen they arrived in Madrid five days before their wedding, Anna was swept up in a storm of activity. Sebastian's mother had made appointments with dressmakers, lace makers, lingerie makers from Paris, boot smiths, milliners, cobblers, furriers; Anna's schedule was full from morning until night. Sebastian had been honest about his background, but Anna had not been fully prepared for the extent of his wealth and his family's powerful position. Naturally, it was a situation to which she adapted with remarkable speed.

On their third night in town, while playing a game of whist in the drawing room after supper, she watched Sebastian smile innocently when his mother praised Anna's inherent talent for managing the tradespeople and servants. His two younger sisters were likewise delighted with the soft-spoken blonde woman Anna presented to the world, the woman who seemed to have captured their mysterious brother's heart so completely. Sebastian's father adored her love of Cervantes and Shakespeare. And even as she won the hearts of everyone in his close circle, Anna could tell Sebastian didn't care much about any of that. He was completely focused on their wedding night, leaving her little trinkets and notes letting her know what it was costing him to repress his ardor.

They were permitted to walk unchaperoned each afternoon in the Parque del Buen Retiro. The ever-present Sister Elvira had finally returned to the convent, once she was assured Anna's virtue was secure under the watchful eye of the very formal Condesa de Montizon.

On their first liberated walk in the park, Sebastian confessed that it all felt surreal. After years of garnering nothing but his parents' disapproval, it turned out that she, a supposed slip of a girl, had thrown the world at his feet.

She had worried that the rumors of her illegitimacy were still floating about nearly two decades later, but when they arrived in

Madrid, a sealed envelope was awaiting them. The barrister of her mother's husband, the illustrious Conde de Floridablanca, wrote to impart that on his deathbed the eighty-year-old *conde* had decided to be generous. He hadn't left her a peso, but he had finally given Anna something he viewed as far more valuable: legitimacy.

The piece of paper that declared Anna's paternity was more than enough for Sebastian's parents, who had feared their rebellious son would never find *any* woman to meet his vague but exacting standards, much less a virginal, convent-raised daughter of the aristocracy. Being illegitimate was hardly something new, it seemed, and the de Montizons were more than willing to turn a blind eye to her questionable birthright.

On their next walk, Anna worked up her courage. She wanted to be honest regarding her ambivalence about fulfilling her wifely duty, in the most traditional sense of the word.

They were walking slowly along a winding path near the lake when she finally blurted, "I'm hesitant, Seb."

"You? I don't believe it! What could possibly give you pause? Tell me." Sebastian looked down at her with those knowing eyes of his. His kindness was turning into something precious and reliable.

"I don't feel comfortable doing the actual . . . thing."

She could tell he was repressing his mirth.

"Go ahead and laugh," she said, throwing her arm out in defeat. "I know I'm being entirely ridiculous. But I just . . . I don't know. It's not what I *want* to do, and I don't want *you* to be awaiting that singular act or for us to be dancing around the matter." She sighed. "How is it that I want to do so many things but not that one?" She shook her head. "I'm all in a flurry."

"Anna, look at me." He stopped walking and lifted her chin so she was looking into his eyes. Even so, she tried to avoid his penetrating stare. For all his submission in her arms, he still had a persuasive nature when he chose to exert it.

"What is it?" she asked, her eyes darting this way and that, like a child who was being forced to confess an infraction.

"Whatever we do in the bedroom—or don't do—you will be my wife in every way that matters to me, Anna."

She looked down at the tips of her new, splendidly embroidered slippers that peeked out from the silk hem of her dress near the gravel path.

Sebastian held her chin more firmly. "Look at me, Anna." She lifted her face to his. "You do believe me, don't you?"

"I'm trying, but—"

"But what?" He looked so crestfallen.

"But I fear you will have demands. *Rights*, even."

He reached out and touched the column of her neck with the tip of his gloved hand. "It is you who hold dominion over me," he said quietly. "Surely you must know that by now. Where or how our bodies are joined—if at all—is entirely in your hands. If Pia brings you pleasure, your satisfaction brings me joy."

She trembled at the mention of Pia.

His voice was warm and close to her ear. "I have dreamt of the three of us together. Of both of us pleasing you."

The touch of his glove, the heat of his breath, and the power of his words—the power he was ceding to her—caused a sharp spike of desire in her gut. "Oh, Sebastian. You are precious to me."

"I will do everything imaginable to remain so." When his hand pulled away, Anna realized his touch was beginning to become essential to her. Yes, she had control—he gave it to her willingly, joyfully—but the more he craved her domination, the more she was beginning to crave his submission. Anna smiled at the irony of need as they resumed walking through the leafy paths of the city park.

The day before their wedding, a gift arrived. A long, thin box wrapped in exquisite Italian paper was delivered to Anna's room with a note from Sebastian.

Everything imaginable. Yours, S.

When their wedding came to pass the next day, everyone was unequivocally delighted.

Anna and Sebastian were married in the family chapel in front of the de Montizons' closest family and friends. Most of the guests stayed for only one glass of celebratory wine and then departed. His parents were extremely strict in terms of their religious beliefs, so the nuptials were far more serious than celebratory.

After the small reception, Anna and Sebastian, his two sisters, and their parents enjoyed a delicious family meal, replete with old recipes that had been passed down through many generations of de Montizon women. Anna looked around and realized she had a family for the first time in her life.

Tomorrow, at last, they were set to depart Madrid for Burgos. It would take two nights and three days to cover the distance, but by week's end, Pia would be in her arms. Or perhaps, she hoped, *their* arms. Sebastian made these wild dreams seem so easily attainable, not only because of his wealth or power but because he showed her how it was possible to ask for what one truly wanted. And she wanted Pia. Her heart thrummed with joy as every hour brought them that much closer to one another.

"So, where shall you live, my son?" Sebastian's father asked across the table at their wedding meal. Now that Sebastian had unexpectedly lived up to paternal expectations, the *conde* was quite lenient in terms of the particulars of what Sebastian planned to do with his future. The family owned endless hectares of vineyards in Spain, as well as sugar plantations throughout the Caribbean and two ships that traveled between the two. "Will you go to the New World as you've always wished?"

"That is one option Anna and I have discussed. My friend Marco has recently sent word that he has arrived safely in Cartagena, and the city is ripe with opportunity."

His father nodded his agreement. "I remember young Marco from your school days. Very industrious. He would make a good business partner, I suspect."

"I agree. But first I want to see more of Europe." Sebastian took a sip of wine. "I am taking Anna to London for a few months, then from there perhaps to the Americas. Do you think you will like that, my dear?" He turned to look at her, as if he had nearly forgotten she was even seated at the same table.

Anna flushed with pleasure. She loved playing the part of his shy wife when they were among company. For some reason, it made the demands she was preparing to place upon him in the bedroom that night that much sweeter.

"Yes, my lord." She kept her eyes downcast but caught the *conde* nodding in silent approval of his respectful, obedient daughter-in-law. The older aristocrat raised his glass to his son, man-to-man.

After the meal, Sebastian's mother and sisters showed Anna to the large guest suite that was to be hers and Sebastian's for their wedding night. The three women helped her brush her long blonde hair and change out of her formal gown and into one of the satin lingerie sets that had been sewn the previous week. After they all made sure she was powdered and buffed and burnished to perfection—and that she was seated elegantly beneath the starched white linen sheets and coverlet—they each gave her a single kiss on the forehead and wished her every happiness in her married life.

A few long minutes later, Sebastian entered the room through the adjoining door. He locked both that door and the one leading to the hall. Anna felt a corresponding wave of anticipatory pleasure roll through her when the bolts slid home. Finally, he was hers to do with as she wished.

Watching his deliberate approach across the room—his strong shoulders and powerful legs nearly vibrating through the rich blue silk of his dressing gown—was like watching the world change from a cold, lifeless planet into a garden of Edenic delights. He moved like the prophetic lion, tightly coiled and powerful, but in his eyes she saw the lamb. When he reached the bed, Anna whipped back the sheet and stood up.

"Now our marriage truly begins," she said. "Take off your robe."

Chapter 15

*H*er words sliced through him like a hot knife. Sebastian's muscles contracted in a quiver of anticipation. As she walked toward him, he undid the knot at his waist and let the heavy silk fall from his shoulders to puddle on the floor at his feet. The late-summer night was cool, and the small fire in the grate crackled in the background. Standing naked and vulnerable in the middle of the room, with nothing but Anna's eyes upon him, Sebastian was fully alive for the first time in his life.

"You are so beautiful, Sebastian," Anna said.

He nearly whimpered.

She trailed a single finger down the center of his chest, then lower, down the middle of his abdomen where his muscles twitched on contact, then finally stopping and pulling away right before she reached the thatch of hair around his stiffening cock. The line of her touch stung his skin, as if she had cut him down the middle with a surgeon's scalpel.

He watched her through lowered lids as she circled around him, touching him lightly here and there, wherever it pleased her. "This is how you should always be. Available to me like this." When she palmed the turn of his bare arse, he hissed out a breath.

"Very nice," she whispered. She rubbed him in a soft circular motion, heating the taut round muscles with a constant, firm touch. "Very nice," she repeated.

When she stepped away to retrieve something from her wardrobe, he exhaled, taking a moment to contain his fervor. A few seconds later, he startled at the sound of one quick swipe through the air. The fine, swooping hiss connected with nothing but empty air and his passion.

"Don't forget to breathe, my pet."

His intake of breath tasted like the sweetest water from a clear mountain stream. Then she swatted the small crop through the air again, closer to him, close enough for a small gust to move around his body. She walked in front of him and tapped the riding crop against the palm of her opposite hand.

"I see you received my gift," he said, no longer caring that his voice sounded desperate or needy. He wanted her to see how much he *wanted*. How much he wanted her.

She smiled and narrowed her eyes. He stared at her breasts beneath the thin satin of her nightgown, then lower at the silhouette of her bare legs, outlined in front of the fire. "I did." She stretched out the two words.

"Do you like it?" he ventured.

"I suspect *you* like it."

His breathing was shallow.

"Am I right?" She trailed the soft leather end along his shoulder and down the length of his arm. A trail of pebbled skin followed in its wake. His eyes closed. "Am I right?" she asked again, her voice taking on a hint of menace.

"Yes," he whispered.

"Open your eyes, darling."

He did.

"I have so many . . . ideas." She dragged the stiff length of the crop along the inside of his thigh, then higher so it skimmed the sensitive skin between his bollocks and arse.

His breath thinned, and his cock throbbed.

She moved the crop in a slow back-and-forth motion across his perineum.

His breath stopped.

"I see." She pulled the crop away, and he missed it immediately. She leaned in and kissed him on the lips, a gentle swipe of her mouth over his, far too gentle. He whimpered. "I know, darling, you want me to be *firm* with you." She kept up that maniacal gentleness with her lips, but on the word *firm*, she pinched one of his nipples, and it rocked through him, straight to his cock. He reached up to pull her into his arms, but she wheeled out of reach. "No, no, no. That is *my* wedding present to you."

"What is?" His voice was a mixture of pleasure and a kind of exquisite fear. A delightful, anticipatory, shuddering dread.

"No hands."

"Oh God." His fingers and palms began to tingle, then clenched closed.

"But first you need to undress me. Look and touch all you like. For now."

"Oh God," he repeated, already approaching a level of wordless pleasure. He watched as she set the crop down on the end of the bed, making sure it was precisely aligned with the edge of the mattress. She turned to face him.

"Take your time removing my bedgown, and then set it neatly on the chair by the fire."

"Yes, Anna." It felt so right to obey her completely. He did as she said, kneeling to lift the soft silk up from the hem, then letting his big hands smooth up her legs, over her slightly rounded hips. He paused there, with the silky fabric bunched in his hands and enclosing her waist. He looked up, supplicating.

She smiled at him, then stroked her fingers gently through his hair. He shuddered at her touch. "May I kiss you here?" he pleaded.

She contemplated him, her thumb tracing his brow, his lips. "Would you like that very much, my dear?"

He groaned and inhaled her scent, so close to his face. "Yes. Yes, please."

"You are very good." He still waited for her nod of approval. When she finally gave it, he dove at her, licking and kissing and using his tongue to map every subtle curve and edge of her sex.

Her clit was already hard against his lips, and he loved the feel of her trembling thighs against his shoulders, the feel of silk and skin beneath his clenched fingers. She cried out quickly, with no attempt at muffling her voice, and he strained his eyes up to watch the glorious release pulse through her strong neck, the bite of her teeth into her lower lip. He loved the pull of her small fist in his hair.

He kept licking her slowly, long after the last ripples of pleasure were past. Loving the soft warmth of flesh and slick moisture, Sebastian let his tongue trail the length of her opening.

She pushed his mouth away impatiently but didn't release her hold on his hair. "That's enough," she said in that throaty, commanding voice he adored.

"Yes, Anna." He remained on his knees, holding the silk gown halfway up her body.

"Finish undressing me, Sebastian." She let her fingers fall away from his hair; her arms hung idly at her sides. She looked toward the fire, almost ignoring him, as if he were nothing more than a servant come to help her with her toilette. He loved that, too.

Standing to his full height, he removed the light gown and put it neatly on the chair by the fire as she'd requested.

"Now give me the belt of your robe," she directed.

He pulled the blue silk from the floor and handed it to her.

"Pull the covers from the bed and lie facedown on the bottom sheet, darling."

He groaned and complied, removing the coverlet and then lying with his arms near his side and his legs together. His hard cock pressed into the mattress with poignant agony.

"Wide, Sebastian. As wide as you can go. I want to see you."

And oh God, how he wanted to be seen by her. He spread his legs and arms. "Like this, Anna?"

"Yes, my sweet. Like that." She dangled the silk belt over his back and thighs, letting it linger between the crack of his arse, then lower. He shivered in anticipation. She played with him like that, making his skin pucker and chill in anticipation, for what felt like an eternity. Finally, she drew his forearms together behind his back and tied them neatly with the blue silk.

"Very nice," she muttered, seeming to admire her own handiwork as much as Sebastian himself. She tested the tension and, satisfied, stepped back off the bed.

He heard the *swish* of the crop as it whistled through the air, and he braced for contact. When it didn't come, he relaxed, and Anna laughed right before she swatted the crop across his bare skin. The sound registered before the pain-pleasure did. Sebastian buried his face in the cool linen and felt every muscle in his body begin to melt into a warm, thick honey.

"Oh! Isn't that something?" She touched the stinging spot created by the tip of the crop, tracing it lightly with her fingertip. Then, God save him, she leaned down and dragged the tip of her tongue along the hot mark on his arse.

"Anna . . ."

"Yes, darling? You like that, don't you?" She tapped the crop a few times against her palm, testing its resistance.

"Yes," he whispered.

"What a fine instrument you are." He wasn't sure if she was talking to the crop or to him.

Then she began.

Lightly at first, stinging his smooth flesh with more of those precise, brief swats.

She spoke to him softly, almost as if to herself. "So beautiful." *Swat swat swat.* "Those delectable squares . . ." Six more swats in quick succession. "Look how your skin responds. You are quite incredible, darling." Her breathy praise wove together with the neat rows of immaculate pain along his arse. The heat of her words mingled with the heat of his skin so she became a part of his body, a part of him.

He lifted his arse, begging silently for more attention. She dragged her fingernails across the neat pattern of pain. The lightning bolt of pleasure—the combination of her light scratch across all that seething skin—sent a shock to his core, and he nearly came right then against the mattress.

"Anna!" he begged.

"Don't even consider it, darling," she answered immediately, but with a slow patience that scrambled his brain. She gave him a little harmless spank with the flat of her palm that brought him back from the edge of his release. "I have so much to learn, you know that. I'll make it wonderful for you, but you must be patient."

As she found her rhythm and confidence, she became bolder. Even though his eyes were shut—his senses overloaded with the physical—he could feel her eyes on him, assessing him, and oh, how he wanted to please her.

He writhed in pleasure and near-terror when she lowered the crop closer to his balls, unsure if his fear or desire would prevail. Instead of smacking him there with the crop, though, she squeezed him gently with her free hand while she began leaving more marks along his upper thighs, making those muscles tense and desperate. Her tender fondling was a maddening counterpoint to the brisk whipping he was getting a few inches away.

But he never faltered. He moaned his pleasure but never cried out or begged for his release. She praised him again for his endurance, and he was rewarded when she straddled his back. When she adjusted her position to better reach his shoulders and upper arms, he felt the hot, wet evidence of her own pleasure against the sensitive skin of his lower back. Her pleasure was mounting at the same pace as his, and he had never felt more joyful.

Eventually, he was lost to time. Sebastian would never know how long Anna went on that night, both of them hot and slick with the exertion. The minutes expanded to years and the years contracted to seconds.

When she had tuned his body to a fever pitch and held it there for an eternity, she finally tossed the crop to the floor and ordered him to turn over. He did as she'd asked, his forearms still bound behind him, muscles straining and forcing his shoulders back and his chest forward. His backside and thighs, shoulder blades and hips, tingled with infernal awareness, burning into the linen sheets beneath him. But when he saw her, he barely noticed the searing heat of his own flesh.

Anna burned brighter than anything he felt against his tender skin. He was blinded by the power of her. She was breathing heavily, her cheeks blazing, her long blonde hair falling around her face, slick with sweat in some places and covering her breasts in others. She looked like a Greek goddess, hands on hips, conquering him.

"That is quite something!" she panted out the words between breaths.

Sebastian was too far gone to reply, but his drunken smile must have pleased her.

Her face softened as she crawled up the length of his body, until she was straddling his waist and he felt her hot core against his hard stomach. She nibbled at his ear and along his neck, then whispered, "I feel so alive." The tips of her breasts grazed his chest, and he arched up even more to increase their contact. Her head leaned back as her chest thrust harder against him.

"Oh, yes," she whispered. "So alive."

She pressed her lips against his, kissing him hard and fast.

"Oh, Sebastian . . ." She enjoyed it for a moment, then pulled away. His hands were still bound behind his back, so he was helpless to stop her. She sat astride him for a few seconds, touching his nipples and letting her long hair hang down like a curtain around them. Then she leaned down and sucked and bit his nipple.

He arched up again.

She stopped and sat up. "So many sensitive places on this body of yours. It's like a treasure trove."

"I love when you touch me, Anna." His eyes were closed.

"Turn on your side, sweetheart." She moved so he could do as she asked, then she reached around and undid the belt at his wrists. She massaged the tingling skin, and he felt the release as the muscles in his shoulders and arms readjusted.

After she finished soothing him, she turned her body so her lips were kissing down along his hip, then her tongue was tracing the length of his hard shaft, and her wet sex was near his lips.

She took him fully into her mouth, and he watched the moisture begin to seep out of her swollen folds.

"Oh God, Anna."

She sucked him hard, and he saw the answering flutter in her sex.

"Touch me, Sebastian," she ordered between long hard pulls.

It was as though he'd forgotten he had hands. And a mouth. He gripped her hips and dipped his tongue into her, both of them coiling around one another on their sides, beginning and ending with the most intimate connection of giving and taking all the pleasure they could.

Sebastian's world telescoped into a piercing tunnel of pure sensation: giving Anna her pleasure while she gave him his—demanded his—was the closest he had ever come to heaven.

Both of them exploded in a shared climax of lips and sweat and tongues and grasping desperate hands and guttural cries.

After, in the dim glow of the waning firelight, Sebastian felt Anna rearrange his almost-sleeping body so his head rested gently on a pillow. She got up at some point and returned to wipe off his sweat-soaked body, lovingly cleansing him and then herself with the flannel and water she had warmed in the basin.

He moaned once or twice, then turned on his side and curled into the pillow when she was finished. After returning the used cloth to the basin, he heard subtle shuffling noises, of her picking up his robe and belt and setting them neatly next to her gown on the chair, then the sound of Anna's wardrobe opening and closing as she put the crop back in its case.

When the room had been returned to order, she slipped beneath the linen sheets and settled her front snugly against Sebastian's back. As he drifted to sleep, he felt his heart swell when her small arm draped around his middle, and she kissed his tender back with a sleepy groan of satisfaction.

Chapter 16

hree days later, in the inn at Burgos, Anna was nearly distraught with anticipation. Ever since they'd left Madrid, Sebastian had served as her maid. He loved tying her into her clothes and draping her in obscene jewels. She usually enjoyed the sensual routine and luxurious baubles, but at the moment she barely noticed the cascade of emeralds he placed around her delicate neck.

"Enough! I can't bear another minute of preparation. How much longer until we meet with the abbess?"

Sebastian smiled down at her, adjusting the emeralds.

She reined in her temper. "Oh, my sweet man. Look at you." She rubbed his lower lip the way he loved, then pressed the pad of her thumb into his bottom teeth and tugged open his gorgeous mouth. "I think you will have much pleasure when you finally see Pia and me joined together. Don't you agree?"

He surrounded her thumb with his lips and sucked, humming his agreement. After she removed her thumb, he leaned down to cover her mouth with his. When they veered toward a more heated passion and his hand started to reach under her skirt, Anna pulled away. "No!" she protested, but she was smiling. "You shall not make me shiver again this morning." She smoothed down the front of her silk gown. "The next time I come, I want Pia's lips on me."

Sebastian smiled. "As do I."

She reached for him again, pulling his mouth to hers for another brief kiss. "I do not know how you came to be my husband, or how you find it in your heart to fulfill my strange desires, but I am grateful for you every day." Her fingers rubbed his cheeks and his eyebrows, his jaw and his lips.

He shrugged, looking a bit embarrassed. "I cannot imagine another woman who would satisfy my own strange desires the way you do."

She smiled at that, remembering the way he had arced like a bow last night, as she had whipped him again with the buttery-soft riding crop he had given her for a wedding present. *A very selfish gift*, she had chided. But he'd also given her a complete set of Shakespeare's plays, and he had promised to take her and Pia to the Theatre Royal at Drury Lane once they arrived in London.

"Very well, very well. That's quite enough mooning," she said. "Now, I want you to meet my girl. I want you to love her as much as I do."

"I know I shall." Sebastian put on his gloves and held out his arm to escort her from their room. "Anyone or anything that makes you burst with as much joy as the mere mention of Pia Carvajal—if it is in my power to give, it shall be yours."

Pia sat in the front waiting room of the convent. The small canvas bag at her feet held her meager possessions: a second dress, a night rail, a small locket with a faded drawing of her long-dead mother and father, and a well-loved, brown, leather-bound sketch pad. She felt the rumble of the carriage on the floorboards before she heard it. Six horses. Maybe eight. She had caught a few whispers among the nuns that Sebastian de Montizon was a very wealthy man. Upon the occasion of his betrothal to Anna, he had promised to donate a large sum to the convent in her honor.

Perhaps he was a debauched rake and would die quickly of some hideous disease, leaving a generous stipend for his widow and her quiet maid. The carriage came to a stop and still Pia kept her eyes downcast. The familiar shuffle of the abbess sounded outside the small waiting room. Would she ever again hear that particular mix of keys and fabric and purpose?

The front door was unlocked and a deep male voice spoke. Pia nearly wept when she heard Anna's sweet tones a few moments later. She looked up to see the door to the small room fly open.

"There you are!" Anna cried, clasping her hands in front of her chest.

A tall, powerful man put one large hand on Anna's shoulder. "Please remember we are in the convent, Anna. Lower your voice."

Pia quickly looked back at the bare wood floor, hardly recognizing her former friend and lover in the elegant blonde woman dripping in emeralds.

"Yes, my lord." Even Anna's submissive tone was unrecognizable.

"And you must be Patrizia." The male voice was now right above her. She squeezed her eyes shut and wished for nothing more than to be swallowed whole into the flames of Hell. It could be no worse than this.

"Pia!" the abbess scolded. "Stand up immediately and pay your respects to the gentleman. Where are your manners?"

She rose slowly, worried her legs would not support her. She didn't know where to look. She couldn't bear to see Anna, now the meek handmaiden to her new lord and master. She couldn't bear to see the man who repressed Anna with a single hand on her shoulder. Instead, Pia firmed her lips and curtsied, a small perfunctory show of little respect.

"Pia!" The abbess was torn between embarrassment and fury. "I am so sorry, señor de Montizon. She has lived her whole life within the convent walls—another infant left in a basket, you see, with nothing but a locket. She has not spent any time in the world. Perhaps an older nun would be a better companion for doña Anna—"

"No!" Sebastian and Anna exclaimed in unison. The gentleman scowled at his wife, and something unspoken passed between them.

"You should not have spoken to the abbess thus," he said to Anna. "Return to the carriage at once."

Anna gasped, said, "Yes, my lord," then curtsied and withdrew.

Sebastian reached for Pia, and she nearly recoiled in disgust at the contact. "And you will accompany your lady. I know we will have a period of adjustment." He kept his hold on her upper arm. "But I also know we will have many years of devoted service from you, will we not?"

Pia despised this man and his arrogance. But Anna was alone in the carriage, and this same man was ordering her to accompany Anna there. She despised him less.

"Yes, my lord. I am sorry I was not properly respectful . . . my lord."

"There's a good girl." He released his hold on her arm and smoothed the fabric of her shabby dress. "Now go attend to our lady."

"Yes, my lord." She bent to pick up her small bag and darted out of the room and then quickly beyond into the courtyard and the waiting carriage.

"I trust you will be pleased with my token of appreciation for the good works you are doing here at the convent," Sebastian said as he handed the abbess a leather pouch heavy with gold *escudos*.

The abbess beamed as she took it. Sebastian suspected that she was probably as happy to be rid of two rather excitable young charges as she was to receive such a generous donation. "Your place in heaven is secure, señor de Montizon. We will be saying mass in your honor for the next four weeks."

Repressing a smile as he thought of the very precarious nature of his place in heaven, Sebastian bowed and gestured for her to lead him out of the room. "Very well, then. I shall be on my way," he said at the main doors.

He exited the convent and smiled at the coachman holding the carriage door wide open as instructed. Sebastian was not going to take the chance of Anna and Pia mauling each other in the forecourt under the watchful eyes of the abbess or anyone else who chanced to come along.

He hopped into the carriage, nodded to the coachman to shut the door, and waved to the abbess through the sparkling glass window of the newfangled carriage his father had given them as a wedding present. After they'd driven a few minutes away from the convent and the building was no longer in sight, Sebastian slowly pulled the silk curtains shut and gave the roof of the carriage three firm taps with the top of his cane.

They were not to be disturbed.

Chapter 17

$\mathcal{A}$nna was a quivering wreck. Pia was so altered. She seemed so cold, even now in complete privacy after Sebastian had pulled the curtains and alerted the coachmen and postilions they were not to be disturbed.

She reached a shaking hand to Pia's pale cheek and watched in silent misery as her lover closed her eyes in disgust, as if Pia must force herself to withstand Anna's touch.

"Did I mean so little to you?" Anna whispered, a helpless tear escaping from one eye. The pain of Pia's rejection was ripping her apart. "You cannot even look at me? You are so changed."

Pia—finally, the stubborn loving woman Anna knew—lashed out at her. "So *little*? Changed? *I*? It is *you* who is changed, in your fine clothes and your gaudy shackles—" Pia must then have remembered her new master sitting a few feet away. She lowered her voice and said to the floorboards, "I am sorry, my lord. I must endeavor to be more respectful to my lady."

"Mustn't we all," Sebastian said on a sigh. "In fact, I think she will have you do her bidding immediately."

Anna hid her relief. Pia's fury stemmed from misunderstanding, not a change in her feelings. Anna took off her own gloves and then started undoing the ribbon of Pia's tatty bonnet while her friend stared in shock at Sebastian. "Yes," Anna growled. "You have been very, very bad to greet me in such a heartless manner. I think you need to give me a proper welcome."

Pia looked confused and worried, but a lovely flush was rising up her chest and cheeks. Anna leaned in and kissed her neck, sucking on her rapidly pulsing vein. The taste of Pia's skin after so many weeks apart made Anna burn with pleasure as her lips trailed up her lover's quivering neck.

"Anna!" Pia sounded as if she'd been shocked back into the present. "Y-your husband will see!"

Anna gave Pia one last lick beneath her ear, loving the familiar scent of her, reveling in the nearness of her, then Anna looked at Sebastian and smiled. Her heart was beginning to race at the reality: this powerful man and this delectable woman were hers now. Anna groaned in pleasure at the prospect, then pulled Pia's face toward hers and kissed her full on the lips. With a small, hampered cry of dismay, Pia tried to pull away. Anna released her but only after eagerly tracing her way around Pia's full red lips with the tip of her tongue. "Yes. He will see. He will see every lovely part of you . . ." Anna's chest was rising and falling in time with Pia's. She finished removing Pia's bonnet and began undoing the simple buttons that ran down the front of Pia's dress. "Oh, my darling girl." Anna's breath was hot in her throat; the anticipation of seeing Pia's luscious body once again, with the added excitement of revealing her to Sebastian, had Anna feeling wild and delirious.

Pia was crying by then.

"I love your tears," Anna whispered hoarsely. "You're so lovely and sweet, so upset and confused, but full of tender desire." Anna smoothed her thumb along the ridge of Pia's collarbone, and they both moaned.

"I don't understand, Anna." Pia looked quickly at Sebastian, then back into Anna's eyes. *That's right*, Anna thought, *find your anchor in me.* Anna felt her sex quake. "How can this be?"

"My husband loves me, it seems." Anna sounded pragmatic, but her heart pounded wildly as she busied her fingers with the front of Pia's dress. "He wants me to have everything I wish for."

Anna finished with the top half of Pia's dress and a gasp escaped her. After glimpsing the binding linen around Pia's confined breasts, Anna was overcome with a fierce need to maul her. She yanked Pia's sleeves down so they held her arms firmly in place. "And I wish for you."

She kissed Pia again, lingering to taste and remember the curve and texture of her lips, then dipped into her mouth until Anna felt a hint of Pia's answering desire—tentative tongue, curious lips—but still no surrender. Anna pulled away reluctantly.

"Oh, you sweet thing. Look at you. Lean forward." Anna despised the binding cloth and everything it represented. If anyone was going to bind Pia, it was going to be Anna. But she would bind her in order to transport her to their shared world of pleasure, not to hide her beauty from the world.

Still weeping, Pia tilted her body as Anna removed the binding linen for the last time. "I never want to see this again." Anna threw the fabric onto the floor of the carriage.

Pia started shivering—perhaps from the air against her bare skin, but more likely from the realization that she was now half-naked in front of a strange man. Anna felt Pia's tremor run through her own sex. "Don't be afraid, my love. I've come to save you, as I promised." She soothed and petted Pia to calm her violent trembling. "Or better yet, feel the fear, and let me be the one to assuage it, to carry you through it. Look at me, love. Trust me."

"Oh dear God." Sebastian mumbled. Anna turned to see he was staring at Pia's voluptuous breasts, and probably doing his damnedest not to palm his own rock-hard cock without permission. "Anna?"

She smiled at him and nodded her approval. "Yes, you may touch yourself, my pet."

He let his head fall back against the velvet squabs and undid the front of his trousers, looking at both women through thick dark lashes. Anna held Pia close as she gasped in disbelief when Sebastian pulled his huge, hard shaft out of the confining fabric and began stroking himself in long, casual passes. Anna shuddered, feeling the rhythm of his hand as if he were touching her mound in the same maddening tempo. She turned back to Pia. "He wants us to be together, darling. Isn't it miraculous?"

Pia whimpered and leaned in closer to Anna, but her eyes never left Sebastian's firm hand. Anna could tell she was both appalled and intrigued. "Watch how he touches himself while I touch you. God, how I've missed you." When Anna leaned down and took one hard nipple into her greedy mouth, Sebastian and Pia both moaned at the same time.

Anna laughed against Pia's breast—the joy of her two lovers bringing her close to tears—and then she suckled the swollen tips of each breast, all the while gazing up at Pia to gauge her reactions. As Pia stared at Sebastian's hand working himself, Anna felt Pia's pulse echo in rhythmic response against her lips.

"Anna, stop! I don't understand what he's doing here—"

"He's our husband, my love." Anna sat up, missing her lips against Pia's breasts as soon as she broke contact.

"Our husband?" Pia's head swiveled from Anna to Sebastian and back again, as she tried to pull the bodice of her dress back into place. "You mean, *your* husband."

Anna leaned in, forcing Pia to stay her nervous hand motions, and placed warm, wet kisses up her neck until Anna was close to Pia's ear. "No, my sweet, I mean *our* husband."

Pia's breathless confusion was making Anna raw with lust; she wanted nothing more than to get Pia to the edge of what she could endure—and then toss her over the edge into glorious release. The poor thing was strung so tight, she was likely to break.

Anna certainly hoped so.

"It's not possible," Pia's voice was getting frantic. "It doesn't make any sense!" She was trying to fasten her bodice, and Anna gripped her wrists forcefully.

"Pia!" Anna used her most dictatorial tone, brooking no opposition. "I have come for you! Stop looking at my jewels and my carriage and look at *me*. Look at me!" She grabbed Pia's face in her hands, digging her fingers into Pia's scalp and pulling her in for a kiss that left no room for thought or worry.

After a few minutes of assaulting her in that way—breaking down her walls of fear and bewilderment with unadulterated passion—Anna finally felt the delectable softening, the familiar way that Pia bent toward her, a flower to her sun. *Complete surrender.* Anna's world melted and realigned, her soul felt complete once more amid the hot flood of mutual desire—give-and-take, power and submission—that had finally been restored.

Pulling away from Pia's mouth at last, all the while stroking her neck and shoulders to make sure she remained calm, Anna looked to her husband and narrowed her eyes. "Sebastian?"

"Yes, my dearest." He kept up the tight-fisted rhythm and looked up from her swollen lips to meet her gaze.

"Please help me show Pia how happy we are to see her." Anna looked into Pia's eyes, absentmindedly fondling one breast and then the other. "Would that be all right, my love? If Sebastian and I both pleasure you here?" She squeezed one of Pia's nipples and then weighed the full breast in her hand. "So beautiful . . ." she whispered.

Shaking her head from right to left as if she were trapped on a hangman's scaffold that could drop out from under her at any moment, Pia stammered, "I want you, Anna . . . of course I do, but I'm so confused. I've m-missed you so—"

"And I you, darling. He knows." Anna raised her head up so she was close to Pia's ear, kissing the sensitive skin in an effort to kiss away her doubts. "He knows everything about us, and he wants me to be happy. He wants *us* to be happy. Do you understand, my dearest?"

"I don't." Pia looked from Anna to Sebastian. Anna smiled as she watched Pia, obviously trying not to stare at his hard cock—and failing—then quickly turning back to look into Anna's eyes. "He is not cruel to you? He does not . . . force himself . . ."

Leaning her head back and releasing a laugh, Anna finally said, "Only when he has been very, *very* good. And even then, it is usually I who exerts the most force."

Pia shook her head again, but Anna knew from past experience that her trepidation was being subsumed by desire.

"Let me show you." Anna wanted to fulfill every dark, unspoken promise. "Let *us* show you."

Sniffing back her tears, Pia nodded. "I trust you. Please touch me again, Anna. Please." She looked at Sebastian and then quickly back to Anna. "You're absolutely certain you trust him?"

"I do. Completely." The truth of it warmed Anna's insides. She did trust him completely; it was a joyful realization. "He wants to love you too, my dear. Will you let him?"

It was probably cruel of her to enjoy it, but Anna thrilled with power as she watched Pia wrestle with her lingering feelings of doubt and consternation. Did she trust Anna enough to put herself entirely in her power, even if that meant being touched by this man, this stranger?

Anna stroked Pia along her neck and shoulders.

"Yes," Pia said on a breath, barely audible. Anna loved her so completely in that moment.

"There's my sweet girl. I adore you, Pia." Anna kissed her tenderly on the lips then turned and looked over her shoulder. "Come taste her rosy flesh, Seb. She can come just like this, from my mouth on the tips of her sensitive breasts. I've been dreaming of how she would delight in two mouths."

Sebastian was on his knees in a second, reaching gently for Pia's left breast while Anna licked and teased her right. Pia gasped at his touch at first, then moaned into the undeniable pleasure of it. Anna bit on the nipple in her mouth and guided Sebastian to mimic the same pressure and pain. Pia cried out, panting and wrestling with the imprisoning fabric of her sleeves that prevented her from touching Anna in return.

Keeping the stiff nipple lightly between her teeth, Anna looked up at her flushed lover. "You remember the rules."

Pia nodded frantically.

"Tell me, darling."

"I'm not to move."

"And?"

She cried out when Sebastian started sucking her nipple deeper into his mouth.

"And?" Anna repeated.

"And I'm not to let go until you give me permission."

"Yes, my love."

Anna dipped her lips to Pia's breast and then reached under the folds of her old dress. Pia cried out when Anna's fingers began to pinch and toy with her hard clit and swollen folds. Anna moaned into the pleasure of it all: the scent of Sebastian, the sound of his rough masculine breathing near hers, the familiar texture of Pia's hot flesh against her lips and fingers.

She wanted to push Pia hard, to make her release become the culmination of all their time apart, the beginning of their future together. Pia was beginning to buck into Anna's hand.

"Shhh, my sweet." Anna withdrew her wet finger and put it into her mouth, the scent and taste reminding her of the elegant wines she was starting to enjoy with Sebastian. "I want to savor our reunion."

"Oh God, Anna!" Pia was close, but Anna wasn't nearly finished.

Desperate for more of the familiar taste and feel of her, Anna closed her eyes and sucked hard on her own fingers. When she was done licking them clean, she whispered, "Oh, how I've missed you,

Pia," her voice guttural. She stretched up to give Pia another hot kiss on the mouth, then told Sebastian to return to his seat.

"And, Sebastian," Anna added without looking at him, "you are not to touch yourself again until I say."

"Yes, Anna."

She looked over her shoulder at him, how he had the palms of his hands resting obediently on his hard thighs, while his straining cock thrust up from between his legs.

Pia was panting, mouth agape, chest rising and falling in anticipation. "Anna . . . please . . ."

"Lie back, sweetling."

Pia obeyed. Anna crawled up onto the velvet seat and lifted the skirts and petticoats fully out of her way, exposing Pia's silky moist flesh so Sebastian had a clear view of Anna's mouth and Pia's sex. "Sebastian, can you see how beautiful she is?"

Again, Pia and Sebastian groaned in unison, and Anna felt as though she were conducting an orchestra. Dipping her head, Anna licked Pia's hot center with a single, prolonged stroke. "Is that better, darling?"

Pia started whispering *please more please more please more*, and Anna felt her own breasts throb in time to the words.

"Only a few more minutes, my love . . . I've missed you . . . I want to show you how much . . ."

"Minutes?" Pia cried out, her thighs shaking, her voice pitched beyond recognition.

Pia's head thrashed from side to side as Anna continued to taunt her, at first with light licks and cool streams of air, then with more purpose. She trailed her tongue greedily around Pia's swelling petals but deliberately avoided the powerful suction and thrust of her tongue she knew Pia craved.

"No!" Pia cried out. "You are cruel." Her body begged for more—hips pitching off the seat and legs flinging wider to give Anna better access.

"Did you miss me?" Anna reached up and stroked the sensitive skin above Pia's pubic hair. Back and forth, Anna lightly caressed her as she watched the pale smooth skin ripple in response.

"Yes," Pia whimpered. "So much."

"Will you always love me?" Anna asked as she trailed her hand through Pia's hair and pinched her clit, then soothed it with the flat press of her tongue.

"God help me, yes!"

Anna pulled away and smiled up at her, then turned her head to nod at Sebastian. "Take yourself hard, Seb." His hand flew to his cock, grabbing it almost viciously as he watched Anna lower her lips and face to feast between Pia's widespread thighs.

When Anna caught a glimpse of Pia's face, Pia was staring at Sebastian's hard knuckles as they fisted taut around his glossy-tipped cock. Anna loved how Pia was rocking into her, her body desperate for release.

Anna slowed for a moment and pulled her lips away. "Now, my sweet. Come for me now." With that, Anna sucked and hummed and drove Pia's body over the brink of ecstasy.

Pia's orgasm crashed through her, causing her head to bang against the side of the carriage and her body to writhe and buck against Anna's lips and hands where she was trying to hold her down.

Anna heard Sebastian's moans of release, and the vibration of his cry shot right to her core. Nearly growling, she moaned in consummating delight when her lips and tongue found Pia's throbbing center once again. She licked and probed, loving the sound of the other woman's desperate begging.

"It's too sensitive! You must stop!"

But Anna would never stop loving her; she would never stop. "Come for me again," Anna moaned into her wet folds. And Pia did, pulsing and fluttering against Anna's lips. Her screams of ecstasy were muffled, probably with a fist or forearm, the way Pia had always done in the convent. Still Anna licked and kissed her, more gently this time. Cleaning her up, taking every bit of her sweetness.

When Anna opened her eyes and looked above the folds of fabric that she had shoved around Pia's waist, she started laughing in sheer delight. "How marvelous!"

Sebastian was kissing Pia and pressing one of his strong hands against one of her bare breasts. He pulled away quickly when he realized Anna was staring at them.

"I'm s-sorry," Sebastian stuttered. "I c-couldn't help it."

Pia was touching her lower lip in shock.

Anna lifted herself up and crossed over to recline along the forward-facing seat, slowly pulling up her own voluminous skirts and spreading her legs to reveal her moist, swollen pussy. Pia groaned with a mixture of surprise and lust.

Anna had not worn underwear since her wedding night. She and Sebastian were so frequently touching one another, neither of them saw the point. Ever so slowly, Anna started rubbing her wet folds in that leisurely way that drove Sebastian mad.

He raked his hands through his hair. "Oh God."

"Do it again." When neither of them moved, Anna's voice turned imperious. "Kiss each other . . . now!"

Chapter 18

ebastian was torn. He lived to obey Anna, but he hated the idea of pushing Pia beyond the boundaries of her desires. He had watched closely as Pia battled her fears and worries a few moments before, finally capitulating and putting herself entirely in Anna's care. But with Anna across the carriage, he wasn't so sure. Perhaps Pia was willing to do things with and for Anna that she was—understandably—not yet willing to do with him. The last thing he ever wanted was to make a woman do something against her will.

In that moment of wondering, Pia looked at his mouth then into his eyes. She licked her lips slowly and nodded her consent, a silent but clear invitation.

He fastened onto her sweet mouth. When he had first kissed her, while she was crying out her release, her response had been so unexpected, so hungry. He hadn't been able to help himself. When Anna had finally given Pia permission to come—then thrust her face between Pia's widespread thighs to ensure that result—Pia had opened her mouth to scream, and Sebastian had felt an animal need to capture it.

She'd responded so beautifully—so naturally—sucking on his tongue as Anna sucked on her small bud, licking his lips as Anna licked hers below. When she came again, her mouth had tasted of the metallic hint of blood, the undeniable physical spurt of fever and want. And he had been lost in it, in the heady scents of two women mingling with his own musk, all of it wafting around him. As he continued kissing her now, he shivered at the realization that these two beautiful creatures had let him into their special domain.

"Oh my," Anna whispered as she shoved a third finger into herself and bucked against her palm.

Pia and Sebastian stopped kissing and held fast to one another as they watched Anna cry out her release.

When she was finished, Sebastian let go of his hold on Pia and went to his knees in front of Anna. "May I?"

"Pia?" Anna asked.

Pia looked up, having been momentarily distracted with setting her bodice back to rights and adjusting the skirts of her dress to cover her legs. "Yes?"

"Is it all right?"

Sebastian turned to look over his shoulder, watching as Pia comprehended what Anna was really asking. Anna had confessed to Sebastian that she'd not kept her word, that she had broken her promise to Pia when she'd allowed Sebastian to taste her and bring her pleasure like that, on that first day in the library at Badajoz. Anna had been too selfish to deny herself, then or since. And Sebastian now felt like a shoddy accomplice for taking his own pleasure in that way, all the while knowing it would hurt Pia when she found out.

Pia's face clouded with the realization. Sebastian admired the core of steel in this woman. She loved to submit to Anna's lovemaking—obviously—but he suspected she never confused that with submitting to Anna's will.

"You have already broken your promise to me, haven't you, Anna?"

The spell was broken.

"You have already let him do what you promised only I would do, isn't that so?" Pia's voice was even. Strong.

Anna sat up straighter and pushed her skirt down to cover herself. Sebastian suspected it was one of the few times he was ever going to see his wife consumed by real shame. Sebastian lifted himself up, quickly buttoned the fall of his buckskins, and then sat quietly on the bench next to Pia. He tried to tuck himself into the corner as best he could, to remove himself from the conversation.

"Answer me." Pia's voice held an authority that was completely at odds with her dark, innocent beauty. Sebastian had thought she looked like some sort of tender earth goddess—full and generous— when she was in the throes of ecstasy. But when she was angry, she was more like a mountain—immovable.

"Yes." The single word from Anna's lips sounded to Sebastian like the most abject apology. A single tear trailed down his wife's cheek.

Sebastian tried to make himself invisible. Which proved impossible.

"And you!" Pia raised her voice and pointed at him. "Did you laugh at me? Did you make her cry out like that, with your tongue and your lips, and think how useless I was?"

"Pia! No!" Anna cried.

"No," Sebastian whispered, staring into her stormy eyes. "If anything, I was jealous of you."

Pia's head pulled back in confusion. "*You*? Jealous?" She barked a laugh, then changed her voice into something akin to a courtly butler. "The great gentleman from Madrid! The wealthy and powerful Sebastian de Montizon! Heir to countless hectares! Jealous of an orphan!"

"She adores you," Sebastian continued quietly. "She usually cries out your name when she is with me." Anna was shaking, weeping softly. Sebastian yearned to comfort her, but he knew it was ultimately between Pia and Anna. "She may not deserve it, but Anna craves your forgiveness, Pia. And I see now, I must beg for it, as well. Please forgive me. I am deeply sorry for any hurt I've caused."

Hanging her head and staring at her clenched hands, Pia stayed silent. Her face was still clouded with frustrated anger when she looked up at Sebastian. "I accept your apology."

The thick silence let him know Anna would not be let off so easily.

"Do you forgive me?" Anna asked after many minutes, her voice cracking on the last word.

Pia finally looked up, staring at Anna through narrowed eyes. "Oh. I'm sorry. Did you apologize? I must have missed that portion of the discussion."

Sebastian wanted to cheer, but he pulled his lips into a tight seam instead. He was going to love this woman and her whiplash understanding of Anna's faults and foibles.

"You know I am sorry," Anna tried.

"Not sorry enough," Pia snapped. "You are too easy on yourself, Anna. We all know you are strong and willful." Pia sighed finally. "And wonderful."

Anna smiled slightly.

"But let me have a few moments to weigh all of this. You owe me a proper apology."

"But didn't I show you how much I missed you?" Anna teased, licking her lips.

Pia smiled, then frowned. "No. I mean, yes. But no! You always show me with your body, but sometimes you need to say the words, Anna. You get away with too much. You need to apologize to me with words; I need to hear the regret in your voice, so I know it's true. Otherwise, it will be one more contest you secretly believe you've won."

Anna was properly chastised. "I am deeply sorry, Pia. I was in a mess of confusion, and then . . . I was . . . selfish. Especially after Sebastian told me he would send for you, that we would all be together . . ." Anna shrugged helplessly. "I felt like everything was resolved. In my mind, we were all three together."

"Well, we were not."

"I know!" Anna was getting angry. "I'm sorry!"

Pia smiled. "You are such a child sometimes. You can't bear to admit when you are wrong. Simply say it."

Into the yawning silence, Anna finally mumbled, "I was wrong."

Sebastian was no longer able to repress his smile.

Anna shot him a quelling look.

"I didn't say anything!" Sebastian said, but he couldn't wipe the smile from his face.

"I was wrong," Anna said clearly, looking straight into Pia's eyes. "I beg your forgiveness."

"There," Pia said, smoothing her dress. "Was that so difficult?"

Anna laughed. "Yes! I hate it and you know it! Don't you remember how I despised confession? As if everything I ever wanted was wrong, every inclination, every desire? Wrong. Wrong. Wrong."

"I remember," Pia said gently. "But I am not your confessor, Anna. I am your closest friend. I love you."

"You're going to make me cry again," Anna said with a peevish tone, as if crying were an inconvenience.

Sebastian watched the two women, watched as the forgiveness settled between them.

"Come here." Pia gestured to Anna, patting her lap. "I want you in my arms when he makes you come again."

Anna smiled and switched seats. Pia spread her legs apart to create a space for Anna to settle her back against Pia's front, both of them fully clothed and looking at Sebastian expectantly.

"Make her cry out for me, Sebastian," Pia said softly, obviously unaccustomed to telling another person what to do. Her hands were roaming over Anna's bodice while she spoke, and Sebastian felt the heat slam into him again. All thoughts of forgiveness and apologies evaporated in the haze of sensual promise.

He leaned forward slowly, lifting Anna's emerald silk skirts and petticoats. He kissed his way up her pale thigh as Pia's hands continued to trail lightly across the swell of Anna's small breasts and the bare skin of her chest.

Anna reached one hand behind her and wrapped her fingers around Pia's neck, letting her fingers grip the hair at the base. When Sebastian's lips touched her pussy, she bucked. Pia pressed down with one strong hand on Anna's hips. "Let me watch him," Pia whispered hoarsely.

Groaning into the restraint of Pia's hold, Anna's other hand reached for Sebastian's dark curls. When her orgasm finally tore through her, Anna's hands clenched with fierce possession, tangling into both of their scalps. Pia and Sebastian locked eyes as Anna cried out. The connection between them was powerful and immediate; their shared love of Anna was something that would bind them together for the rest of their lives. Pia kissed the side of Anna's neck as the final waves of her release pulsed through her, never taking her eyes from Sebastian's. *We will both love her*, that look seemed to say. And the thought swamped Sebastian with an entirely different—more profound—satisfaction.

When he pulled away from Anna's sex at last, his lips and chin still moist, he lifted onto his knees and leaned up to kiss the sweetness into Pia's mouth. She closed her eyes and took it, and he could tell she was loving the taste of Anna between them, loving the admixture of all three of them.

Then Pia withdrew from Sebastian and tilted Anna's face to bring her lips to hers.

"All three of us in one kiss," Anna whispered in profound wonder. She adjusted her position so they were able to settle into each other's arms, then each of them slipped into a gentle slumber as the carriage rocked along the north road toward Bilbao, where they would board the packet to London.

Chapter 19

The trip to Bilbao lasted many hours. Pia awoke first. She untucked herself from Anna's loose hold, where she'd fallen asleep against her chest. She moved to the other seat to avoid waking either Sebastian or Anna. Amid the usual bounce and rumble of the carriage, her change in position did not cause Anna to stir. Sebastian, on the other hand, was awake in a flash, his hand reaching for his sword beneath the seat. When his eyes cleared enough to remember where and with whom he was, he smiled gently and slid out of Anna's hold to join Pia on the forward-facing seat.

Pia pulled aside one of the curtains to look out across the passing landscape. She gazed at a range of mountains to the west, purple and majestic in the fading light of dusk, then let the curtain fall back into place.

"So beautiful." She turned to Sebastian. "Do you know this part of the country?"

"I do, actually. Those are the *Montes Obarenes*. Even though I grew up in Madrid, Javi and I went to university in Pamplona."

"And you and your friends spent much time in the countryside in this region?"

He looked skeptical. "We did."

She nodded; it was more than enough information to draw the conclusion she'd been forming.

"What do you know of the countryside?" Sebastian pressed.

She smiled. "You can put your tongue on my breast, your lips on my mouth, but you think it ill-advised to give details of a political nature to a mere miss. I understand."

They were both whispering so as not to wake Anna, but if Sebastian's surprised look had been given voice, it would have been heard from a mountaintop. "What do you understand?"

She shrugged and continued whispering. "I understand that, at the convent, we used to leave food and other basic provisions at the edge of the garden for . . . people . . ."

"And?"

"And . . . I have heard Javi's name mentioned," Pia continued slowly. "I don't know if it is the same Javi, but . . ." She shrugged again. "I am nearly invisible to many people. I am a parentless charity case of no consequence. People tend to speak freely in my presence. As if I were a deaf-mute."

He reached for her hand. It wasn't a seductive touch necessarily, but it was warm and made Pia trust him. "And you've remembered every word, I suspect?" He rubbed her knuckles in a lovely back-and-forth way.

"It's exhausting keeping it all in." She leaned her head back against the velvet squabs and closed her eyes as she spoke. "But the abbess and the older nuns, they are powerful. They are landowners or mothers of landowners. Sisters and widows of powerful men. They are aristocrats. They are mothers of kings. Grandmothers of queens. Daughters of dukes, like Isabella."

Sebastian brought Pia's hand to his lips and kissed her lightly.

"What was that for?" she asked, opening her eyes and turning to look at him.

"I don't know." He smiled at her. "Anna's been so excited—distraught really—about what would happen when we came to get you." He looked down at their joined hands. "I'm relieved, I suppose."

Pia pulled his knuckles to her lips this time. "I am also relieved." She set their hands in her lap gently. "I thought . . . terrible things about you."

"Like what?"

"I thought you would be cruel and domineering."

He stifled a laugh.

"I know. Silly, yes?" Pia blushed.

"Yes," he replied, then his voice turned more somber. "But perhaps it is to be expected if that is what you have heard of men and their treatment of women."

She nodded, glancing across the luxurious carriage at Anna's delicate features pressed against the velvet squabs. "Isabella used to talk to us about how we should try to fight harder for our independence, and we would all look at her as if she were crazy." She turned back to face him, continuing to speak in a low voice, just loud enough to be heard over the rhythmic clatter of the horses. "She may as well have suggested we go work in the garden without breathing any air. Anna especially would challenge her."

"I got to know Isabella fairly well when we were traveling to Aveiro."

"Really?"

"Yes. She can be single-minded."

"Well, she can *afford* to be single-minded, can she not? What with her fortune."

"Yes and no. There are plenty of women with fortunes who still defer to the wishes of others for their whole lives. I do not think you or Isabella or Anna are cut from the same cloth as most women today."

"That may be true." She was silent for a few moments. The roll and sway of the carriage lulled her, made her want to be more candid with him. "Although, I do not think I am cut from the same cloth as either of them. Both are fierce in their ways."

"Perhaps. But I think you, too, are fierce in your way. Mindful in a way that Anna is not. Powerful."

She nearly choked out a disbelieving laugh. "Powerful? What a strange word to use to describe me. The clothes on my back and a small canvas sack constitute the entire expanse of my dominion."

Sebastian smiled, and Pia had the strangest feeling. Again, it wasn't lust, though there was that still unfamiliar frisson of physical attraction in it, but something deeper and more far-reaching. He felt like an ally.

He tapped the side of her head. "Your power is here. You remind me of Javi in some ways. You collect information. I can see it in your eyes." He stroked a finger across her forehead. "Your wealth is here. I am interested to see how you will use it."

"Use it? How can I? I am nothing."

He squeezed her hand. "Ah. That is where you are wrong."

"What do you mean?"

"You are about to be surrounded by the most elite members of London society. Men will approach you and want to dance with you at balls. You will be pursued. I have a wealthy friend who is going to introduce us into his circle. These are important times in the corridors of power. The New World is still so new. Lives are being made and lost all the time."

Pia felt a combination of fear and delight. "I thought I was to be a lady's maid. Do lady's maids attend balls and dance with gentlemen in London?"

"You were never going to be a lady's maid," Anna said. Pia startled at the sound of her voice. "Tell her, Sebastian," Anna ordered with a sly smile, stretching her arms until she touched the gray fabric of the carriage roof then letting her hands rest in her lap. "Go on. It is such a delightful plan."

Pia smiled at Anna, then turned her full attention to Sebastian. He was quite enjoyable to gaze upon, after all. Having spent her whole life in the company of women, many of whom had been manipulated by male members of their families, Pia had expected all men to be harsh and brutal, like the traveling priests who said mass at the convent on occasion. Brutal or, at best, dismissive.

While there was something vicious about the turn of Sebastian's jaw when he clenched it, a deeper compassion and love flowed from him in a seemingly endless supply. He had a generous soul.

"Yes," Pia whispered. "Tell me."

His eyes lit as he began. "We shall enter London society as the aristocratic houseguests of the Most Noble Farleigh Edward, Duke of Mandeville."

"Oh my. He sounds dreadfully fancy. Is he a friend of your father's?"

"No"—Sebastian beamed—"he is only a few years older than I am. Thirty-two, I believe. We met the year before last, when he was part of a British delegation in Madrid. He took an interest in the . . . efforts upon which Javi and I had embarked."

Pia looked from Sebastian to Anna and back again. "Well, am I to be included in these exciting affairs of state?"

Anna laughed and reached for Sebastian's hand across the area of the carriage that separated them. "I told you she would be thrilled. Won't she be the most delightful spy?"

Sebastian smiled but shook his head as he released Anna's hand. "I told you, darling. There's to be no spying."

"Oh, you know what I mean. Intrigue! Excitement! Allow us a bit of enthusiasm, Seb. Think of where we've been for the past few decades. Compared to the convent, walking through Hyde Park will feel downright sinful. Don't you think, Pia?"

"Oh, I do. I am so—" All of a sudden she began weeping again.

Anna knelt in front of her instantly. Sebastian leaned over and put an arm around her shoulders.

"What is it, my sweet?" Anna pleaded, reaching her palm to Pia's cheek to console her. "What has saddened you?"

She lifted her eyes to look at Anna. "I am not sad. I believe I am overset with joy." She started laughing through her tears, and Anna reached up and kissed her gently on the lips.

"I know," Anna soothed. "I cried myself to sleep for many nights while we remained in Badajoz. I couldn't quite reconcile myself to the truth of our freedom." She looked at Sebastian, then back at Pia. "But we are free, darling. We truly are."

Pia inhaled deeply. "There. I feel better again." She patted her tears away with a small handkerchief. "I suppose I must prepare myself for these crushing tides of happiness. Who would have ever suspected I would need to become accustomed to such a thing as joy?"

Sebastian brought his lips to Pia's cheek for a brief kiss. "I believe you shall become very accustomed to it, my dear."

Anna sat back in her seat and smoothed the silk of her skirt as the carriage rumbled along the dark night road. "So, tell her the rest, Sebastian. I love hearing you talk about all these important personages."

"Yes, do tell me," Pia added, reaching tentatively for Sebastian's hand again.

He smiled and squeezed her hand in his. "Very well then," Sebastian continued. "Once we are settled in London, we will make the acquaintance of one Lieutenant General Arthur Wellesley—"

"A fast-rising member of the British military," Anna hastened to add.

"Yes, he is that," Sebastian agreed. "And then we merely need to deliver a message from Javier to Wellesley. Quite simple really."

"Oh, you're far too modest, Seb," Anna scolded. "It's very important, Pia, in order to root out that interfering Frenchman who thinks he can ride roughshod over all of Europe."

"Well, I suppose that is true." Sebastian looked thoughtful as he gazed out at the passing terrain. Pia liked the way his thumb slid across her knuckles as he collected his thoughts. "Spain is ours, after all. If we are able to convince Wellesley to redirect his troops to the peninsula, he may very well be able to help those of us who are, shall we say, unhappy about Napoleon's recent arrival."

"Do tell the rest!" Anna looked as though she could barely contain her enthusiasm for her new political purpose.

Sebastian turned to Pia and spoke openly and directly. In a way she'd never dared hope any man would speak to her: honestly. "If we can convince Wellesley to postpone his military adventures in South America and return to Portugal instead, we are certain he can cut Napoleon off before his influence is too widespread. Ever since Bonaparte's arrival in Spain, Javi and the rest of us—the younger generation as it were—have been eager to find a way to ally ourselves with the British. With the vacillating allegiances of everyone from the Portuguese to the Italians, the Russians, and the Danes, it is imperative that we secure the loyalty of the English at the earliest possible moment."

Pia nodded her understanding. "I agree with my whole heart. Please let me know how I can help."

Sebastian reached for her cheek. "Anna knew you would want to."

Again, Pia sensed in Sebastian a deep connection, like a comrade-in-arms, but the way he touched her so tenderly, the way he spoke to her with respect and kindness, also made her uneasy.

"What is it?" he asked, clearly sensing her hesitation.

"I simply never thought I would meet a man who treated me as his equal. It's so . . . unanticipated."

Anna clapped her hands together in delight. "Precisely! I didn't believe him for a minute, poor thing. He had to explain himself again and again when he proposed. I was that convinced he meant to bully and intimidate me."

Sebastian blushed, and in that moment, Pia thought he was the most loving man on earth.

The three of them spent the final hours of their journey going over the specifics of Pia's new identity, that of an eligible, well-dowered young Spanish woman entering London society under the auspices of Farleigh's powerful mother, the widowed Duchess of Mandeville. Throughout their animated discussions, Pia saw how Anna watched Sebastian. She seemed to love him without realizing it. Anna smiled when she looked at how Sebastian held Pia's hand or spoke in that soothing way of his.

Through some miracle, after the long carriage ride and the nights on the road, followed by the rough sea voyage from Bilbao to London, there didn't seem to be a hint of jealousy between the three of them but rather an abiding trust, a growing interdependence. They all warmed to the new and exciting adventures that awaited them, especially Pia and Anna, after having been cloistered for so long.

Chapter 20

When the small boat arrived in London, Pia nearly kissed the slimy wooden planks of the dock. "Never again!" she cried.

Anna and Sebastian had nursed her throughout her violent seasickness over the course of the entire journey.

"How will we ever get to Cartagena, my love?" Anna asked, trying to make light of her ill humor. They had spent many hours onboard the ship talking about where they would go after England, what parts of the world they would explore.

"I shall never survive it. You two will have to go without me."

"Unthinkable," Sebastian soothed, as he helped guide her along the crowded wharf. "Either we all go or we don't go at all."

After he had helped Pia to more solid ground, he looked up at an ornate carriage emblazoned with what could only be the seal of the Duke of Mandeville. A liveried servant jumped down from his seat atop the gleaming carriage and pulled open the door. A tall blond gentleman stepped out.

Pia watched Sebastian's face light up as the man approached, and then turned to see Anna's face clouding. Before she had a chance to remark upon Anna's reaction, Pia was swept up in the swell of Sebastian's enthusiastic cry.

"Leigh!" Sebastian called. "You shouldn't have come to the docks to meet us. We are dreadfully tired and probably look a fright."

As the blond man neared, Pia could see more clearly that he was stunningly handsome. Her seasickness must be wearing off because she thought he might be the most beautiful man she had ever seen. He radiated a classical perfection. A perfectly straight Roman nose, alert light-blue eyes fringed with dark lashes, and a lush mouth that looked quite sinful, almost feminine. But the wide turn of his jaw was utterly masculine and harsh, a perfect counterpoint to those sultry lips.

He and Sebastian were the same height and build—strong shoulders tapering to muscled hips—so when the duke pulled Sebastian into a rough hug, Pia had a moment of unexpected excitement. The idea of two men . . . like that . . . would be . . .

"Quit gawking," Anna growled.

"Oh." Pia looked modestly back to the ground, then decided she was not obliged to look away. Anna might control her when they were intimate, but Pia had no intention of submitting to her every whim. She pulled her hand from Anna's forearm and crossed her arms defiantly in front of her chest.

Sebastian was laughing and talking in English with his old friend. They'd become acquainted during the duke's visit to Spain as a British envoy two years ago, but by the look of their obvious pleasure at reuniting, Pia was beginning to suspect Sebastian and Farleigh had been far more than acquaintances. Or perhaps that was her lust-addled brain playing tricks on her. Still, something about the way their eyes glinted and widened when they spoke to one another put Pia in a heightened sense of awareness.

"How rude of me!" the duke said in perfect Spanish. He bowed and took Anna's hand. "You must be Lady Anna de Montizon." He kissed the back of her glove.

Anna stiffened and withdrew her hand. Pia smiled inwardly at the prospect that Anna might be experiencing her first pangs of marital jealousy. The duke knit his brows momentarily and then turned his attention to Pia.

His blue eyes sparkled. "And you are Patrizia Carvajal?"

"I am, Your Grace." Pia gave him a small curtsey and dipped her chin.

"And do you also dislike when a duke kisses your hand?"

Anna's nostrils flared, and she walked the few steps to stand by Sebastian.

"It depends . . ." Pia said with the slightest hint of a smile.

"On what does it depend, my lady?"

"On the duke, of course." She held out her hand as she said it, offering it to him for a kiss. She caught a glimpse of Anna's stormy expression, and it stirred something rebellious and sensual inside her.

A few moments later, after the luggage had been secured, the four of them stepped into the duke's closed carriage. The sheer size of the city was overwhelming enough, but the onslaught of sounds, smells, and streaming, packed humanity had both women staring out the carriage windows with wide, unblinking eyes. From the crowded docks of the Thames Embankment, through the teeming streets near the river, into the loud thoroughfare of Oxford Street, they gaped. As they passed near Bloomsbury, the duke mentioned something called Montagu House, where he promised they would all go visit a treasure of recently acquired artifacts, including the Rosetta Stone and the Townley collection.

Pia squeezed Anna's hand for a moment at the idea of so many grand discoveries, and her friend turned to smile in shared wonder.

"It is truly magnificent, is it not?" Anna asked.

"It is." Pia smiled and was glad their wordless squabble at the dock was forgotten. Despite Anna's intensity and subtlety when she was physically intimate, Pia had always known that her friend was rather a dolt in other ways. Anna was a wonderful listener, but she had to be focused on whomever it was she was listening to; she did not often see the subtle interactions of others unless they were rather glaringly put before her. In Anna's complete absorption with the city's splendor, for example, she had completely missed the byplay between her husband and the duke.

Farleigh and Sebastian were sitting on the rear-facing seat in order to afford the ladies a better view. Ostensibly.

Pia was now sure the two men simply wanted to sit next to one another so their strong legs and shoulders could jostle together as the carriage made its way through the huge city. The prospect—real or imagined—of those two men being lovers had sent Pia's already-full mind into a veritable roil.

Perhaps she had simply become a voluptuary after so many days spent in close confines with Anna and Sebastian, the three of them barely able to keep their hands off one another even in the communal areas of the packet ship. The only time Pia hadn't felt utterly nauseated was when one or both of them had held her in their arms or touched her with more intimate affection. As a result, maybe everyone with whom she became acquainted would forevermore be reduced to some sort of physical possibility in Pia's sex-addled brain.

While Anna continued to stare out the window in silent wonder, Pia tried to steal surreptitious looks at those strong male thighs tightly constrained within finest buckskin. It was blindingly erotic, all that muscle barely disguised beneath a layer of taut leather. As she watched through dipped eyelids, Farleigh's hand rested casually on Sebastian's thigh, then squeezed the hard muscle. Pia's eyes flew up, and both men smiled at her.

She blushed and looked out the window—caught in the act, as it were. Without thinking much about it, she squeezed Anna's hand, keeping it in hers as they continued deeper into the city and then on into the green spaces of Mayfair.

As the carriage drew to a stop in front of an immaculate brick town house on a quiet, leafy lane, Farleigh gave Sebastian a rough slap on the cheek and said, "Come on, old chap!"

Pia could see Sebastian's cock twitch in his tight trousers in reaction to that seemingly friendly thwack.

Oh dear, oh dear. Pia was in a whirl. Anna was staring out the window in amazement. Sebastian was staring at Pia with a knowing look in his eye. He knew she would love . . . what? To watch? To touch? As the two men wrestled one another like a pair of ancient Greek warriors. All that flesh and muscle, rubbing and sliding.

Oh dear.

Farleigh peered back into the carriage over Sebastian's shoulder and asked in elegant Spanish, "Ladies, will you be coming inside then?"

"Oh!" Anna said. "Is this where we are to stay?" She turned to look at Sebastian, who quickly looked away from Pia.

"Yes, my love." Sebastian extended his hand in a courtly manner to assist his wife. "Let me help you from the carriage." Sebastian took her hand and helped her to the cobbled sidewalk.

Pia took Farleigh's extended hand, and the four of them entered through the brightly painted red door that was being held open by a servant splendidly attired in full livery of a matching shade of outrageous red, trimmed in gold.

Farleigh squeezed Pia's arm to get her attention. "Would you like a cup of tea or to go to your rooms to freshen up?"

"I would like to rest, if that's acceptable. It's been such a long few days."

"Of course. It's been a long journey. My man will show you up."

Pia nodded at the duke, then reached out to kiss Anna on both cheeks and smile at Sebastian. "Until later, my friends." As Pia followed the butler, she turned at the first landing of the elegant stairway to glance down at the three people in the front hall. Pia had the sense that Anna and Farleigh were about to engage in some sort of biblical battle that would grant the victor eternal power over Sebastian's beautiful body.

arleigh gestured for Anna and Sebastian to precede him into the drawing room.

"Please, go ahead. I'll just be a few moments, if it's not too rude. I've something I need to attend to before I join you both for refreshments."

"Of course," Sebastian said easily. "Take all the time you need. Anna and I will be perfectly content until you return."

Anna followed Sebastian into the elegant room, and he was startled to hear the latch click shut behind him. He turned quickly to see her standing in front of the closed door. She looked so formidable; even travel weary and exhausted, she projected a coiled power. Sebastian's heart pounded with each step he took toward her.

"Do you want him?" Anna asked softly, barely enunciating the words as she brought her fingers to his cheek.

For a moment, his eyes closed in pleasure when her palm caressed his face. Then he looked at her, taking her measure, and spoke carefully while he leaned into her comforting touch. "Somehow I don't think you will have the same reaction I did when I asked you a similar question about Pia in the library at Badajoz."

Anna furrowed her brow and looked down at the lovely tea that had been laid out on a spindly round table to her right. "You have trapped me."

Sebastian took her hand away from his cheek and held it in his. "How, my love? I have never done anything to trap you. I thought I offered you every freedom."

She looked like she might cry.

"Do you fancy a turn in the garden?" Sebastian asked. "Perhaps we should speak alone."

When she looked up into his eyes, he was taken aback to see the most supplicating emotion emanating from deep within her powerful, dominating lover. He realized in that moment that regardless of her fervor in bed—or maybe because of it—she appeared to be quite ill prepared for emotional intensity.

Sebastian released her hand as he reached to open the door to the hall. "Farleigh?" Sebastian called.

The duke turned from the conversation he was having with one of his subordinates and replied, "Yes? Do you have everything? I'll be there in a moment—"

"No, no. The tea looks splendid, but Anna and I wish to take a turn in the garden. Will you excuse us?"

"Of course, of course," Farleigh said with a deep voice and an accommodating nod. "Fresh air is what you need after your journey. The doors are unlocked, and it is a lovely afternoon. Take your time."

He returned his attention to the servant without a further glance, and Sebastian pulled the door shut to afford them more privacy.

"Shall we sit here or do you fancy a bit of fresh air in earnest?" he asked.

"Perhaps we should take a turn outside," Anna said on a sigh. "The softness of that silk sofa puts me in a mind to ravage you, and I think I must do the hard thing for once and speak my mind rather than indulge my senses." She smoothed the fabric of her practical traveling gown, then reached out for Sebastian's hand. "Come, my pet."

He did not take her hand but reached out slowly and wrapped his arms around her waist, nuzzling into her neck and pulling her close. "I am happy to indulge your senses after you speak your mind . . ."

She moaned into him, both of them responding to the pressure of his erection against the softness of her belly. "You are so lovely, Sebastian. But after." She set him away from her and slid her hand onto his forearm. "Please take me round the gardens."

He opened the French doors that led to a surprisingly large walled garden behind the house. The enclosure had been cleverly designed to create hidden spaces within tall walls of greenery. A willow tree created a verdant cave. A pergola dripping in ancient lilacs offered another secret meeting place. Sebastian kept leading her away from the house. A large pine tree, gnarled and thick limbed, concealed a small bench that faced a charming little waterfall at the back corner of the garden. The small trickle of water cascaded endlessly into some sort of fountain that had been made to look like a mossy, rocky riverbed.

"How's this?" Sebastian asked, pulling aside a pine branch so Anna could duck and take a seat.

"Lovely," Anna said as she sat down on the bench.

"Yes, it is. Now—" Sebastian sat beside her and turned her chin to face him. "—tell me what you are thinking."

"It sounds so hypocritical. I'm not sure I can say it out loud without hating myself a little." She looked up to the sky—or what remained of it through the shady pine branches—and Sebastian couldn't resist trailing his finger along her neck.

"I adore you, Anna. You know that, don't you? I will do whatever you wish."

She turned slowly to look at him. "Tell me your true feelings."

"I love you." He spoke the words without hesitation.

She shook her head and stared at the pine needles beneath her feet. "That's not what I mean."

"Look at me, Anna." When she didn't respond, he added a quiet, "Please."

She looked at him but stayed silent.

"Are you asking if I have feelings for Farleigh?"

She firmed her lips but made no move to answer.

He waited her out.

Finally, she whispered, "Yes, that's what I'm asking."

He took a deep breath and exhaled slowly. "I do."

"Oh God." Anna looked toward the main part of the garden, twisting her body away from him as if she might be able to escape if she stretched hard enough.

"Anna?"

"Yes?" she answered, without turning to look at him.

"I don't need to act on it. I was being honest because, well, I always *am* honest with you. I don't know how else to be."

She turned then, and he finally saw the depth of affection in her eyes—all calculation and hesitancy gone, with only pure love remaining. He wanted so much to pull her against him, but he knew she was still battling her own feelings, or coming to admit them at last.

"I will do whatever you wish where Farleigh is concerned." He almost laughed at the idea. "Really, you must know that I will do whatever you wish where *anyone* is concerned. Don't you see that?"

"Oh dear. I hear your words, but I cannot quite grasp the truth of them."

"It seems I am forever convincing you of my honest intentions."

She reached for him—*finally*, it felt to him—and he pressed his hand over hers where it lay against his pounding heart. Keeping her close.

"Why didn't you tell me before now?" she asked, sounding almost hurt.

"What was there to tell? That I had a bit of a romp with a man. Would it have shocked you?"

She shook her head. "I'm selfish, not a hypocrite. I don't care that you were with a man—I can hardly have a thing to say on that score, given my own history with Pia. But . . . your feelings are something else entirely. Perhaps it is that I now find myself a guest in his house that I am at a disadvantage. It seems like I should have known beforehand."

He sighed. "Truly, I was quite certain the spark had died out. But . . ." He looked at her lips and her cheeks, then back into her eyes. "But it seems he still stirs something in me."

"But—"

"But nothing, Anna. Just because I have a frisson of renewed attraction to someone I once knew in that way, does not mean I am untrue. Or ever will be. I will always be loyal to you. In fact, if you would rather we stay elsewhere, at a hotel perhaps—"

"No . . . I . . . just give me a moment to collect my thoughts. It's not jealousy, precisely."

"Then what is it? Whatever it is, I don't want you to feel the least discomfort."

Anna's forehead drew together in concentration. She was absently rubbing his chest, smoothing the fabric of his jacket, while she appeared to be clicking through the possibilities in her mind. "I'm curious," she said slowly. Sebastian held his tongue, unsure if she was going to ask the type of brazen question she was wont to ask—namely, *how was the sex?*—or if she was going to talk about her own feelings on the matter. "So . . . if I said I was . . . it was . . . fine with me . . . if you made love to Farleigh again . . . then you would?"

A bit of both, he thought with a smile—her feelings, his sex. Her boldness in stating it outright sent a flush up his neck and cheeks.

"Only if you were completely at ease with it, my love," he answered at last, when he realized she was waiting for his reply.

"And if I asked you *not* to?"

"Then I would not." He said it so quickly and with such conviction, there was no way either of them could deny the truth of it.

"But you would never ask me to give up Pia . . ."

He narrowed his eyes. "The thought would never cross my mind. It's true, I would never ask such a thing of you."

"So then . . ." She looked so adorably flustered. "Why . . . how can you be so free with me?"

Sebastian laughed, low and almost to himself. He looked at the ground, then at his hand over hers. "Because your happiness is my happiness," he said softly. The truth of it filled him with a thick, hot desire.

"Oh my."

He looked into her eyes. "And if my being with Farleigh—as lovers or in any other capacity—would make you unhappy, then that would make me unhappy, too."

"I am so confused. I don't want to be so selfish. But, oh, I am the most selfish creature!" She clamped her small hand into a fist and punched her own thigh. "I would worry." The tears came then.

"Oh, my dear," Sebastian reached to touch her neck, and she used her shoulder to shake off his offered comfort, as if she were not worthy of his kindness. He put his hands back in his lap. "What would you worry about?"

"That he would do things for you . . . " Anna stumbled over the words. "That he . . . is better . . . that he has things . . . the thing . . . I cannot provide . . ."

"Oh, my love!" Sebastian pulled her into a hard hug, despite her resistance.

She tugged at his hair and pulled his head down to hers. Her lips were harsh and punishing against his soft ones. She bit and tore at his mouth, as if she wanted to mark it permanently as hers. "You are mine," she growled, pulling his hair harder until he moaned in blissful agreement.

She reached between them, and he felt the resistance of his erection against her palm. "Undo your trousers," she ordered.

He pulled away and had the buttons undone in mere seconds. He dropped to his knees, the blanket of pine needles cushioning him. "How do you want me, Anna?"

She put two fingers in his mouth, and he sucked them desperately, his eyes barely open, his tongue twirling around.

"I want you inside me," she whispered.

Sebastian almost came right then. His eyes flew open. "Are you sure? What has changed your mind?" He continued kissing the palm of her hand, then along her wrist.

Anna smiled softly. "For some reason, it no longer feels like a capitulation but rather the sharing of some mysterious power." She ran her free hand through his hair. "Your body is mine to explore and enjoy." His eyes drifted closed in anticipation of all that entailed. "If I don't enjoy that particular act, then so be it," she said pragmatically. "But I'm quite finished having a fixed opinion about something I've never tried."

"You're certain?" he asked, then began kissing her fingertips.

She removed her hand from his lips and pulled up her skirts to reveal her neatly trimmed pussy. "I am certain."

"Tell me what to do," he pleaded, his voice rough with anticipation.

She started touching herself with fingers still wet from his mouth, spreading herself open in that contemplative way that drove him to distraction, lazily tracing the slick evidence of her own desire. "I want to ride you. Lie back, my sweet." She stood up from the bench, holding her skirts bunched around her waist, and gestured for him to recline on the pine-scented earth.

Everything about their fecund surroundings and her languorous movements was primitive and natural. Sebastian was overpowered by a profound and soul-soothing communion. Keeping her skirts hitched up in one hand, she straddled his body and began to lower herself onto his cock. Her moist sex touched the crown of his, and then she pulled away an inch.

He groaned in desperation.

"And of course, it goes without saying that I must come before you," she declared. "Will you be able to hold back?"

"I will do everything in my power, but you are so beautiful."

She smiled that powerful smile down at him and reached out to touch his lower lip. "So are you, my love. So are you."

He reached for her then, and she shook her head.

"Tsk tsk. Hands above your head, Sebastian."

He stretched his arms over his head with a plaintive sigh.

"Don't worry, my dear," she said as she taunted the tip of his cock with her wet folds. "I will make sure you are properly secured next time."

He nearly cried out at the words, throwing his head back at the glorious prospect that there would be a next time.

She slid down onto him, slowly and painstakingly encompassing every inch of him. She was using him in the most rudimentary, fantastic way. Her eyes were closed and her hands were fluttering, one around his face and one between them, along his straining shaft. He was swept away by her touch but forced himself to keep his eyes open, to see the intensity of her experience.

"It's so warm." She spoke like a scientist, dictating notes to a class of students who were observing a rare undiscovered flower for the first time. "So much more subtle than I'd imagined. The veins and the tender skin . . ."

"Anna." Sebastian was nearly beyond speech, her name filling him to the exclusion of anything else.

Then she began to ride him, gently at first, in that meditative fashion, slowly tilting this way or that, trying him and testing him to suit herself. Then she found her rhythm and used his body mercilessly.

"Anna!" he cried out. She covered his mouth with her small hand, and he licked her salty skin desperately, needing her touch and her permission. Needing *her*. "Please!" he cried against the skin of her palm.

She threw her beautiful blonde hair back, and her inner walls gripped around him, so tight and fierce, so like her. "Now!" she cried, and he flew over with her, his cock throbbing and his balls clenching as her glorious orgasm extracted everything from him, every part of his soul flying into her keeping.

Chapter 22

h my." Anna was splayed out on Sebastian's chest, her cheek pressed against the clean white linen of his shirt, his heart pounding steadily into her ear. "That was beautiful."

"Yes, it was," he whispered, his voice filled with awe. "May I touch you?"

She breathed him in. "Yes."

His hands came down lightly on the sweaty fabric along her back, trailing reverently to her narrow waist then across her bared bottom. She felt the skin prickle beneath his adoring palms.

"What we have, Anna, it is something—"

"Shhh." She rested her fingertip against his lips. "I need to say more."

"Please."

"I think the most . . . the hardest part for me to face . . . is that I've fallen in love with you, Sebastian. That I love you."

He pulled her into a tight hold, both of his arms flying around her narrow waist and keeping her firmly against his body. She had never said it, and obviously he was overjoyed to hear it, if his reaction was anything to go by.

"Why is that hard to face?" he asked finally. "I find it wonderful to love you so much. I want to tell you all the time."

"You love *love*, Sebastian. You exude it." She kept her face turned away, resting her cheek against his warm, solid body. "For me, love is the terrible thing that destroyed my mother, that led her to do all those devastating things—to disobey her husband, to throw her life away."

"Anna?"

She looked up after a few more seconds, resting her chin on the backs of her hands. "Yes?"

"What if your mother was glad she did what she did?"

"What do you mean?"

"What if the Conde de Floridablanca and the nuns and everyone up until now made you *believe* your mother was miserable and full of regret? But what if she loved the British man who fathered you? What if things had been different and she had lived to bring you here, and the three of you had lived as a happy family?"

She smiled at Sebastian, thinking how innocent he was in certain ways. "So many what-ifs, my sweet Sebastian. Your mind always takes such a happy turn."

His body moved beneath hers as he shrugged against the pine needles. "Life is full of surprises, my dear. I ɔok at us. I never thought I'd marry, much less fall in love. I dreaded an eternity of my father's disapproval and having to live a secret life to enjoy my . . . proclivities . . ."

Anna smiled at him.

"And instead of that? I got you, all rolled into one: my demanding mistress, my tender lover, my devoted wife."

She turned her face to the side again and sighed. "I know. We are lucky. We are so lucky. I only meant . . . love makes me feel unstable, a little weak."

"Only a little, I'm sure." Sebastian laughed, and she reveled in how it thrummed through her, how his happiness underpinned her own.

And there it was. The realization that she wanted *him* to be happy. That she did not need to be the sole *source* of his happiness. That she would revel in his happiness as he reveled in hers.

"Oh fine. Only a little weak," she conceded.

They rested like that for many minutes, their breathing taking on a shared rhythm, their bodies pressed together. A while later, Anna sighed again. "I may as well confess all . . . since I've managed to break every promise I ever made to myself in my youthful, prideful ignorance . . ."

"What promises have you broken?" Sebastian interrupted, stroking her hair away from her eyes.

She tapped his chest as she enumerated. "One: I promised myself I would never fall in love with you. Two: I promised myself I would never come to rely on your love. Three: I promised myself I would never enjoy being, well, penetrated by a beastly man."

He laughed, and she saw the love in his eyes and the way her words worked him into that state of bliss.

"I can't say I'm sorry you broke any of those promises." He continued rubbing a strand of her hair between his fingers, and she shivered as the small gesture sent a thrilling jolt down her spine. "So what else are you confessing? Other than how irresistible you find me."

She gave him a light punch on the chest, and he laughed again. After a few seconds, she looked him in the eye, all seriousness. "I must confess . . . I am far from ambivalent about your attraction to Farleigh—"

"Honestly, if you are opposed—"

"I want to see you and Farleigh together. It stirs me even now to imagine it . . ." Her inner walls tightened around his softened cock, still inside her. "But I'm too much of a coward to confess it."

"I think you just did."

She laughed, and it felt free and liberating as it rang through the secret garden. "I believe I did." Anna stretched to kiss him on the lips. Oh, how she loved this wonderful man. How she thrilled to the idea of seeing him taken in hand by that English Adonis. "When?" she asked, breathless and eager.

It was Sebastian's turn to laugh again. "I think, for once, I am going to make *you* wait."

Anna pulled away quickly, then smiled wickedly. "Oh, it's worth being punished for, is it?"

"Quite." His eyes narrowed. "I think perhaps we should go to a ball, or a concert, someplace wonderfully formal and public, all buttoned up and repressed. And you shall have to bow and curtsey and be held at arm's length. And you shall see how Farleigh and I will touch each other, man to man, nothing untoward, riding in the carriage, discussing the horses, enjoying one another's manly company."

Anna felt her heart speeding up. "Yes . . ."

"Or perhaps we should have a fencing match or few rounds of boxing . . ."

"Perhaps . . ." Her hips were beginning to rotate against his stiffening cock. "Would it be very sweaty?"

His lips curved at her interest. "It is midsummer—" He flipped her onto her back and lowered his lips to hers. "It would be a sweaty, panting mess." He began moving inside her as he continued intermittently taunting her with lurid descriptions of Farleigh's slick, muscular body wrestling against his. She dug one hand into his thick black hair and grabbed the fabric on his upper arm as she screamed into his kiss when he made her come again.

Chapter 23

For the next two weeks, nothing was said of sensual possibilities, though much was implied. Farleigh was getting testy.

After the four of them spent the first night at Farleigh's home having a quiet, restorative supper, they were hurled into a social tumult.

The Spaniards excited a *furore*.

While in Madrid, Anna had ordered a complete wardrobe for Pia, as well as one for herself. The two of them struck quite a chord when they entered the ballrooms of Mayfair—Anna petite, rigid, blonde, and cool as a winter wind, and Pia tall, voluptuous, and dark as a raven's wing.

And Sebastian.

Farleigh watched across the crowded ballroom as Sebastian spoke to an elderly woman who was standing next to Farleigh's mother. The way Sebastian engaged the dowdy shrew so completely, responded so animatedly, made Farleigh smile. As soon as Sebastian turned his attention to someone, that person inevitably believed she was the center of his universe. Ladies sighed and seemed to melt as he passed nearby, and gentlemen sniffed around for an introduction in order to set up boxing matches, fencing contests, and other tests of physical prowess.

Sebastian had been in town for only two weeks, and he already held the cream of London society in the palm of his hand. Of course, Farleigh wasn't jealous; it wasn't in his nature. He was far too pragmatic for jealousy. But . . .

It would make Farleigh's life far more *enjoyable* if Sebastian stayed on for a longer visit. He was quite good company, always amiable. The idea of an indefinite visit was most enjoyable of all—especially when Farleigh was alone in his room at night, thinking over the turn of Sebastian's shoulder when he threw a right hook or the straining thigh muscles in his buckskins, taut and firm as they were now in his breeches, shadow and sinew accentuated by the candlelit chandeliers.

The last thing Farleigh had expected when he'd received word from his newly married Spanish friend was that their physical attraction would ratchet higher upon his arrival in London. In fact, Farleigh had been expecting an utterly boring married couple. The affair between Farleigh and Sebastian in Spain two years ago had been nothing more than a youthful foray. An itch to scratch. But Sebastian had changed since then. Farleigh often found himself unable to look away from the strapping, confident man he'd become.

Yes, Farleigh had taken full advantage of Sebastian's submissive proclivities two years ago—the pleasure Sebastian took in being taken, as it were, was a natural fit for both of them—but Farleigh had assumed Sebastian's acquiescent tendencies would have been erased, or at least tamped down, now that he had decided to take the traditional route and marry a young Spanish convent girl.

How wrong could Farleigh have been! Watching the way Sebastian nearly melted at his wife's smallest demands, Farleigh was even more titillated upon realizing Sebastian's submissive nature had also matured. If he could have him like that, entirely at his mercy—

"You'd best stop mooning over him or someone will begin to suspect," Pia said softly as she brought a small glass of ratafia to her lips.

"No one would ever possibly suspect anything," Farleigh said, without taking his eyes off Sebastian's perfectly muscled behind.

"Why is that?"

"Because everyone knows I'm in love with you."

Pia sighed and exhaled through her nose. "You must begin disclaiming such false reports."

He turned and looked at her spectacular face, long and proud and utterly unfoolish. "The reports are not entirely false, dear Pia."

"Think how many poor girls in this very ballroom—and their mamas—would give their eyeteeth to hear such an enthusiastic declaration."

He smiled at her sarcasm and lifted his chin. "I've no need of eyeteeth, you know that. And neither one of us is much for exaggeration or flattery."

"That much is true." She returned her gaze to the dance floor where Anna was once again swirling about with the very attentive Arthur Wellesley. "You have no need of anything, Your Grace. That much is clear."

He narrowed his eyes and refocused them on Sebastian who had turned to scan the room for his friends. When he spied Farleigh and Pia, his face bloomed into a fabulously inappropriate smile, and he began heading toward them through the crush of guests. "I used to think so, Pia. But now I'm not so sure."

"Ah. I see," she answered softly. "I feel sorry for your future wife."

"Why is that?" He looked at her intently.

"Oh, please, don't let's mince words. Any potential wife will never be able to compete with your feelings for him." She lifted her chin in Sebastian's general direction, smiling when she saw he was waylaid once again on his journey toward them.

"Is that so?" Farleigh prodded, drawing her into the trap.

"Of course that is so. It doesn't take a clairvoyant to see you're attached to him or . . ." Her voice faded.

"Or what? I like the sound of your self-righteous conviction. It's so refreshingly unladylike."

"Very well then. You're in love with him. How is a wife supposed to compete with that?"

"The same way a husband does."

"I beg your pardon?"

"You heard me. The same way Sebastian competes with you for Anna's affection."

"There's no competition between the three of us—" Her gloved hand flew to cover her mouth.

"Aha!" he said, loud enough to draw a few turned heads from the area where his mother was sitting with some of the older doyennes. He lowered his voice. "I suspected as much. You three are, in fact, *three*. Am I right?"

"Farleigh!" she whispered hotly, then lowered her hand and schooled her features to bland disinterest. "Pardon me, Your Grace, for speaking in such an appallingly familiar manner."

He smiled, enjoying himself in a ballroom for the first time in living memory. "Patrizia!" he said in a tone of outraged surprise that mimicked hers.

Her face blushed furiously, and he had a brief glimpse of what it would be to make love to her, or better yet to make love to Sebastian while Pia watched them with those stormy eyes of hers that never seemed to miss a speck.

"Duke." She tried to sound stern, but he could tell she was beginning to simmer. "We are in a ballroom." It was impossible to live in the same house for two weeks and not feel the burbling desire that fizzed and popped around Sebastian, Anna, and Pia. Farleigh wasn't absolutely certain what their arrangement was, but he was intrigued.

And getting hard.

He thought about a bucket of icy water being thrown on his groin and got his lust back in check. "So we are, Lady Pia. So we are." She looked at him quizzically. "In a ballroom, that is."

"Oh, that. Yes, we are."

He was quiet for a few more seconds, then asked, "The truth is all rather promising, isn't it?"

"I don't think I follow."

"I want it to be four." He stated it plainly, as if he were placing an order for a new set of neckcloths from Mowbray's.

"Farleigh!" she whispered harshly. "You mustn't speak so in public. These are potentially criminal offenses not to be bandied about so blithely." She kept her eyes on Anna and the flirtatious lieutenant general in his absurd red coat as they whirled around the floor.

Farleigh shrugged. "Funny you should mention the illicit aspect of my sordid nature. As it turns out, the situation becomes far *less* criminal for me with you and Anna hanging about nearby."

She pretended to ignore him.

"And you *would* be hanging about, wouldn't you, Pia?" He touched her elbow with his, and he thought he felt her shiver. "I know how observant you are, such a keen eye for the smallest detail."

Pia groaned at his provocative words. He was right, of course. The idea of watching Farleigh and Sebastian had nearly consumed her with lust over the past weeks. The two men bantered all day long, patting each other on the backs, or that one time, when Anna had been out in the garden collecting roses, when Farleigh had smacked Sebastian's bottom as he left the room. The two men were always jolly and *physical*. Fencing. Boxing. *Sweating*.

All the while, Pia's temperature had been rising to dangerous levels through no physical exertion whatsoever. She was often flushed and fluttery. Idiotic, really.

The days were foolish enough—the four of them attending at-home visits about town or taking rides in the open carriage through Hyde Park—what with all that *proximity*. But the nights were far worse. After midnight each night, Pia slipped unnoticed from her guest room into Sebastian and Anna's bed in the adjoining suite. The three of them enjoyed a tender and consuming passion, and also the simple comfort of being exactly where each of them wanted to be. At home in one another's arms.

Sometimes Anna was the center of attention, bossing Sebastian around and pulling Pia's lips to hers. Other times Pia was spread wide, wrists and ankles fastened to the four posts of the tester bed, while Anna and Sebastian licked and sucked and rubbed and cupped and tormented her body until she was begging and begging and crying out. Anna had taken to gagging her with a strip of leather Sebastian had commissioned for precisely that purpose. It seemed they were not alone in their proclivities, Sebastian having discovered a rather accommodating leather smith who was quite adept at making all sorts of anatomically correct *toys* out of the softest hides, polished wood, and finely honed metals.

And of course, there was Sebastian, that delectable creature who wanted nothing more than to please Anna and, by proxy, to ensure that Pia and Anna were left utterly satisfied whenever it was within his power to make it so.

Pia was not a greedy person. Or at least she'd never fancied herself greedy before now. She was ever grateful. She knew full well she had more love and physical satisfaction than most people ever dreamt possible—much less experienced!—in the course of a life spent battling hard, cold reality.

Still.

Lurking in the back of her mind—and, she suspected, in the front of Sebastian's and somewhere around the perimeter of Anna's—was the idea of Farleigh. The idea of Farleigh in the same house in his own large bed, quite alone, while the three of them were finding solace and joy in each other, was beginning to nip at Pia's conscience. It seemed a shame.

He was probably only a few yards away, if one were to remove the walls.

Pia had undertaken the demolition project in her mind many days ago. When Anna licked her or Sebastian toyed with her breasts, Pia shut her eyes and pictured Farleigh there. Sometimes he was across the room, casually holding a glass of whiskey in his strong fingers as he did in the drawing room, exuding all that blasé confidence. Other times he was standing closer, near the edge of the bed, tracing her mouth or the curve of her ear while the other two made her body arch and crack open with pleasure. Farleigh always observed her.

And something about that seemingly clinical act of studied observation had become so exquisitely erotic that the thought of it sent Pia into a weakened state of longing, right there in the ballroom.

"You've thought of it, I see," he said in a low, complicit, throaty voice.

Oh, that voice of his. So prim and filthy all at once. "I have not . . ." She cleared her throat, not wanting to lie. Because not only had she thought of it but she had contemplated every fantastical permutation. She swallowed. "I have not merely thought of it, Farleigh. I've pictured it in exquisite, lifelike detail."

He barked that arrogant laugh again, apparently not caring who heard or whose wrath he incurred. In fact, his inappropriately forward behavior with the mysterious Spanish lady was more apt to bolster his reputation than ruin it. "I applaud your honesty, Pia. I believe I shall convince you to marry me after all."

She exhaled again and held her tongue. Anna was finally finished dancing; she and Wellesley were making their way toward them. The ballroom was crowded, and it would still be many minutes before they were all reunited.

Sebastian had been snared in a gaggle of women consisting of the Duchess of Abbyville and three of her six eligible daughters. Farleigh smiled and raised his glass in a tiny salute. Sebastian widened his eyes in a desperate plea to be rescued from the ever-tightening circle.

Pia had learned that, even though he was married, most mamas saw Sebastian as a potential bridge to the eligible Duke of Mandeville. The fact that Farleigh was notorious for preferring the company of men—in and out of his bedroom—was of no concern to ambitious mothers in the marriage mart. He was titled and terribly rich. Sexual inclinations were the least of their worries.

"I've told him repeatedly he must learn to be more standoffish," Farleigh said, looking at Sebastian in his pickle.

"It's not in his nature to be rude. I know it's difficult for you to understand when someone actually enjoys being pleasant."

Farleigh swung his head to face her. "That is quite a terrible thing to say to your future husband."

"Oh, do stop with that." Pia wasn't able to hold her stern expression for long, especially when his lips curved into his most conspiratorial, intimate smile.

"I like sparring with you, Pia. It's almost like talking to a man."

Pia almost spit out her sip of the overly sweet liqueur. "You know, I think you actually meant that as a compliment." Her eyes were slightly moist from her enjoyment.

"The highest." He nodded and returned his attention to Sebastian, who was finally extricating himself—with the help of Farleigh's mother—from the cluster of desperate women. "Ah, good. Here he comes."

Chapter 24

Sebastian couldn't have been more grateful to Farleigh's mother than he was at that moment. She had proved quite helpful in so many regards, but in social extraction she was on par with a military maneuverer. Pia, Sebastian, and Anna had been presented to Farleigh's mother, the Duchess of Mandeville, at her grand home on Piccadilly the day after arriving in London. The formidable old woman had been more than willing to help implement their plan to get Wellesley to redirect his efforts back to Portugal rather than join forces with de Miranda in the New World. Not that she knew anything about the particulars—she had merely been given the task of introducing the Spaniards into high society, and it was a task to which she was perfectly suited.

While many other matrons had curled their lips at Farleigh's *animated* behavior, the Duchess adored her son and chose to turn a blind eye to his flamboyance whenever other people commented on it. On more than one occasion, Sebastian had observed her skillful conversational deflections. One older man had recently implied that the duchess should take a firmer hand in disciplining her son and show more concern about putting a stop to the rumors that he was engaging in illicit acts.

"Oh, I wouldn't want to disappoint you," she replied without pausing.

"Disappoint me?" the monocled prig asked.

"Yes, I would hate to rob you of such a pleasant pastime."

He was beginning to see where she was headed and shifted uncomfortably. "Pastime?"

"Obviously *disciplining my son* is something you have spent much time contemplating. I shan't take away such a treat." She smiled benignly, and the man's wide eyes and falling monocle were his only response. He tried to sputter a reply, but the duchess merely shook her head slightly. "That is all."

The man had walked away, and once again, Farleigh's mother had prevailed. Even so, Sebastian could see it was wearing on her.

Sebastian suspected she didn't much care what her son did on his own time, in his own bed, but she had a tender heart and was very outspoken in her desire for grandchildren. Sebastian felt the older woman soften, and he looked up to see the direction of her gaze: Farleigh was laughing boldly and was briefly touching Pia's gloved forearm.

"Am I wrong to hope?" the duchess asked.

Sebastian smiled kindly. "I believe one is never wrong to hope."

"I knew I liked you." She looked at Sebastian for a few seconds longer, assessing him.

It occurred to him that this delicate old woman saw right through his social mask to his pounding heart. What had started as a bit of protracted flirtation—spending time with Farleigh to see Anna's keen anticipation of some debauched sexual culmination between the two men—had escalated into full-blown madness. Sebastian was falling in love with Farleigh.

Anna was a genius, he had to confess, by encouraging him to flirt and jostle with Farleigh as much as possible, while never letting them get any closer than a manly pat on the back or that one fabulous swat on his bum. At first, gamboling around Farleigh had been a sweet torture; now Sebastian was at the end of his tether. He reminded himself he was escorting the man's mother across a crowded ballroom and tried to temper his enthusiasm.

"Are you becoming tired, Your Grace?" Sebastian asked the duchess while they weaved through the crush of people who'd formed now that the music had ceased.

"I am. But you young people should carry on. I see your wife has Wellesley sitting in her pocket. Perhaps you should stay for the elegant refreshments Lady Chienjour usually serves."

Sebastian watched Anna, rosy from her time on the dance floor, laughing amber eyes sparkling up at Arthur Wellesley. Sebastian's hand was resting on the duchess's, over where she'd placed hers on his forearm. He must have pressed her hand against his without realizing it.

"There, there, Sebastian. Don't fret, you sweet man. She sees nothing in him."

He breathed through the unfamiliar emotion. Welcoming Pia, or even Farleigh if it came to that, into his relationship with Anna felt like something delicious and sensual and ambitious. Seeing Anna snap and spark while she parried with the likes of Arthur Wellesley felt like something, if not sordid and cheap, at best vapid.

If Anna started experimenting with men and women all over Europe, Sebastian wasn't sure he could remain cavalier. "Oh, I don't fret. Anna sees much in many people," Sebastian replied, trying to sound vague and noncommittal. In a perfect example of ill-timed coincidence, at that very moment Anna happened to look at Pia, and a flash of raw hunger passed between them. It was gone in a moment, but Sebastian could tell that the duchess had seen it.

"Ah. So she does. But it's not the same, is it?"

Sebastian gave up trying to force his way through the packed sea of humanity and led the older woman to a slightly less crowded area near a column at the side of the room.

He and the duchess stood quietly for a few moments. "She is quite animated, that's all," the duchess finally said. "Let her have her fun. She's been holed up in that convent all her life. Let her play a little."

"I'm not sure I'm as much of a libertine as I thought I was."

The duchess thought that was splendid, tipping her head back and laughing with the all-consuming glee that was so much like her son's reaction when he was similarly delighted.

"Oh, Sebastian, I see why he loves you."

Sebastian's head flew to face her. "I beg your pardon?"

"Oh." She opened her fan and slowly, without a hint of unease, began to swish it back and forth in front of her chest and neck. "No one suspects."

Sebastian couldn't repress a smile—Farleigh's sexual antics were legendary.

The duchess smiled back. "I meant no one suspects *you* in particular. Farleigh made such a commotion about that actor last year; the gossip mill really hasn't stopped turning since."

"You are an unusual woman, Duchess."

"Sometimes if you make a few concessions to propriety, you can live a very fulfilling and rewarding life within its supposed confines."

"And you would know?"

"Yes, I would, young man." She slapped her fan shut and used it to gesture toward her wrinkled neck and face. "I wasn't always this prunish, you know. I was quite splendid, really." Her voice was soft with memory, as if that splendid creature had been someone else entirely.

"You are still quite splendid, I think," he complimented, letting his voice take on a slightly flirtatious quality.

She snapped open the fan and smiled, but her voice was haughty when she said, "I almost believe you, but that's no way to be talking to the mother of your . . . very dear friend."

In that moment, Sebastian felt an unspoken benediction: this woman believed in her son's right to his own happiness, whatever path he chose in its pursuit. They looked at one another for a few moments, and she nodded once, barely noticeable, and Sebastian felt all of her kindness.

"There you are!" Anna cried dramatically as she pushed her way past the final row of crowded guests that separated them. Sebastian watched, amused, as Lieutenant General Wellesley was relegated to serving as her adjutant, pulling up the rear as he apologized to everyone she'd cut in her wake. Farleigh and Pia were close behind. "We were all desperate to find you," Anna said breathlessly, looking up into Sebastian's face. Her shining eyes bound him to her as much as any rope or leather.

He bent down slowly and kissed the inside of her wrist. "I was desperate to find you, too," he said softly, so only she could hear, then more clearly. "Did you enjoy your dance with my wife, Wellesley?"

"Very much, indeed. She is quite something."

Sebastian nodded, not liking the satisfied way Arthur Wellesley looked at Anna. "She is," Sebastian said shortly. "Quite."

"She tells me you have news from Javier in Badajoz," Wellesley said as he reluctantly looked away from Anna's flushed cheeks.

Sebastian straightened. It was easier to set aside what amounted to nothing more than petty jealousy when he remembered the fate of the Spanish nation rested in relaying the information to Wellesley. "Yes, sir. Are you available to discuss the particulars tomorrow?"

"I'd rather discuss them now."

Sebastian was unsure whether to respect or disdain this man's arrogant abruptness. Marco and Javi had assured him Wellesley was to be trusted, but Sebastian had his doubts. He set them aside. If Wellesley was able to redirect his troops to Portugal instead of the colonies, he could perhaps defeat the French bastards quickly and thoroughly.

"Very well," Sebastian said slowly. "You wish to speak in front of the ladies?"

Wellesley looked at Anna and Pia, then his glance slipped to the duchess. He bowed slightly in a show of respect. "Your Grace."

"Arthur," she said with familiar ease. She had known him since he was quite young.

"Speak, man," Wellesley demanded quietly.

"Very well," Sebastian began, lowering his voice. "By the middle of August, Delaborde will be near Roliça . . ." He continued recounting the specific details—locations, numbers of troops, the name of a traitor in the Portuguese army—weaving all the particulars together in a subdued, confident voice that was unintelligible to passersby. Meanwhile, Anna, Pia, Farleigh, and the duchess spoke gaily about nothing of any importance, in order to further obscure the nature of Sebastian's report.

Wellesley rarely spoke, merely nodding amiably as if Sebastian were sharing a not particularly engaging tale. When Sebastian was finished, Wellesley nodded once more but gave no other indication he'd registered a single word.

A few days later, Wellesley and nine thousand troops, who'd been preparing for a transatlantic voyage to assist Francisco de Miranda in South America, changed their ship's manifest and headed to Gibraltar to reconnoiter with five thousand more soldiers and then continued on to Portugal to defeat the French. For the time being.

Chapter 25

"It's July and the Season is over," Farleigh declared a few mornings later while he pretended to read the paper. "Wellesley has agreed to change course. Your obligations in London have been met. Isn't that right, Sebastian?"

Sebastian hummed his agreement as he chewed on a bite of ham and eggs.

"Very well, then." Farleigh folded the paper and tried to sound blasé, but Anna could tell he was a cauldron about to boil over. "I suggest we all retire to the country for the rest of the summer."

The four of them were sitting at one end of the long table in the formal dining room in Mayfair, enjoying breakfast. Or at least Anna was enjoying herself. She reached her hand into Pia's lap and said, "Oh, Farleigh, that would be wonderful. Wouldn't it, darlings?" Anna turned to Pia and then across the table to catch Sebastian's eye.

She knew she had become quite careless in her flagrant attention to both her husband and her lover, no longer caring if Farleigh's servants suspected they shared a rather *modern* arrangement. Anna had also realized that the more seemingly outrageous she was with Pia in public, the less people suspected.

When she and Pia had attended a show of paintings last week, for example, it was quite fine for them to hold hands or link arms—almost expected. They were the best of friends, Anna would say, the closest of intimates. When Pia would blush at the double entendre that only she understood, Anna would taunt her further, pointing out how lovely Pia was to anyone who would listen. Of course, the society matrons—and ambitious bucks who were attracted to Pia for both her dark beauty and the large purse with which Sebastian had provided her—would all politely agree and compliment Anna on what a kind friend she was, to be so generous in her praise of another woman.

But at home, here at Farleigh's, she had another motive. By taking all her liberties so openly, so casually, she was heightening the tension between Farleigh and Sebastian in the most delightfully cruel fashion.

"We all three adore the outdoors," she said, finally pulling her gaze away from Sebastian and facing Farleigh. "Don't you?"

"Yes, Anna. I *adore* the outdoors." His peevishness was obvious, but she pretended not to notice it.

"It's so freeing," Anna continued, looking out the window with a dreamy expression. "No confines of society. All that lush grass to lie upon and cool lake water sluicing across one's skin."

Sebastian took a sip of his coffee and exhaled through his nose, obviously picturing all of that lush and sluice.

Farleigh merely growled.

Anna smiled sweetly.

Pia sighed.

If he didn't murder Anna first, Farleigh was going to thank her profusely for the desperate, pliant lover she would present to him when she finally gave Sebastian permission to put himself in the man's power. When they arrived in the country, she had decided, the time would be right. Anna wanted the two men to have complete freedom, and there were simply too many inquisitive servants around the London town house. There was nowhere to escape notice.

Anna had spent much time with Farleigh's mother over the past few weeks, and eventually she began asking the duchess all sorts of questions about their country estate, Mandeville House. The old woman had the fluttering heart of a swooning sixteen-year-old girl and soon suspected the direction of Anna's inquiries. She regaled Anna with a litany of all sorts of suggestions for clandestine meetings: secret bolt-holes, abandoned play cottages in the forest, discreet swimming locations that would permit all manner of folly, and an area of the stable yard that must have conjured wonderful memories, if the duchess's wistful expression was anything to go by.

"How soon can we depart?" Pia asked breathlessly, resting her hand over Anna's.

Oh, to be back in the open air with this woman's body beneath my hands. It was Anna's turn to sigh.

"The sooner the better, I say." Farleigh's voice was irritated and short. He called across the room to one of the footman and ordered their things to be packed at once. "We leave in the morning." He pushed his chair away from the table with a grating scuff and stormed out of the room.

Anna took a slow sip of her tea and smiled over the rim at Sebastian. When he resituated himself in his seat, she set the teacup back in the saucer and said lightly, "No squirming, my sweet. You're almost there."

With the footmen gone to do Farleigh's bidding, she turned to Pia and kissed her full on the lips, then said, "We are going to have quite a show. Don't you think?"

Pia whimpered and reached up to grip the back of Anna's neck, pulling her in for a deeper kiss.

Moving away slightly, without taking her eyes from Pia's, Anna said, "Why don't you go for a ride in the park with Farleigh, Sebastian? I think we all need to blow off a bit of steam." With that, she began kissing Pia again and trailing her hand up Pia's bodice and cupping her breast. As Sebastian was leaving the room, smiling at the two women, Anna called, "Be a dear and tell the footmen Pia and I are going to have a leisurely breakfast and don't wish to be disturbed."

"Yes, my love." Sebastian pulled the door closed with a gentle smile and an erection that Anna could see from across the room.

After the door had closed, Anna kissed Pia once more, hard and quick. "Let's move down to the other end of the table. I've been thinking of having you here."

Anna gestured for Pia to sit atop the far end of the dining room table—where it was clear of dishes and food—then she pulled Pia's legs apart and positioned her chair between Pia's spread thighs. Reaching her hand beneath Pia's skirt and feeling her slick heat, she said, "God, you are so beautiful. Lean back for me." She pushed gently but firmly against Pia's stomach until she was lying back fully, with only her legs dangling off the edge of the table from mid-thigh.

Anna began lifting the layers and layers of petticoats and expensive silk that now constituted Pia's wardrobe. "I almost miss the simplicity of our old dresses."

Pia laughed and reached down to rub her hand briefly against Anna's soft blonde hair. "I don't. I'm almost ashamed to confess how much I already love the feel of satin and fine linen against my skin."

"You do?"

"Yes . . ." Pia's voice faded as she rose up on her elbows and Anna's kisses began to trail up her inner thigh. "Because all that luxury reminds me of your lips," she whispered.

"Oh, darling. What a sweet thing to say. I'm going to have to give you many silky kisses then." She kissed Pia between her legs as an example.

Pia moaned her pleasure. "Please hurry, Anna. Seeing Farleigh and Sebastian getting so bothered has got me all riled, as well."

"Me too," Anna chuckled. "But now I'm very hungry for you, so there won't be any hurrying. In fact, you are going to have to be extra patient."

Pia's head arched back, and a hiss of pleasure escaped her when Anna's lips and tongue began their tender, patient assault on her sex.

Chapter 26

The next day, two carriages were packed and the four of them were on their way out of the city shortly after eight in the morning, Farleigh and Sebastian riding ahead on horseback, the ladies in one of the closed carriages.

Farleigh thought he'd seen a glimmer of amusement in Anna's eyes when he had briskly declined her suggestion that the four of them ride together in the carriage. He couldn't imagine a more irritating prospect than jostling up against Sebastian for the entire nine-hour journey while Pia's curious, encouraging eyes bored into him. If Anna de Montizon had been a man, Farleigh would have killed her—or fucked her—weeks ago. She was making his life a burning hell.

And *burning* was not too strong a word for it. He burned for Sebastian like he'd never burned for any man. The way Anna toyed with Sebastian, the way Sebastian looked at her and obeyed her. The mere thought of it made Farleigh's cock tighten in his trousers.

He kicked his horse harder.

"Relax, man," Sebastian said as they turned the horses into the stable yard in front of the Falcon.

Farleigh had sent word by messenger yesterday that the Stevenage inn should have a lunch ready for their arrival. "I am not of a mind to relax, Sebastian. And well you know it."

Sebastian tried to repress a smile and failed.

"There is nothing humorous about how badly I want you," Farleigh ground out. They had both dismounted and were standing near each other in the empty yard. A stagecoach had recently left and the next had yet to arrive, so they were granted a moment of quiet in the usually bustling yard.

"Farleigh—"

"Don't!" He was still holding his riding crop and swatted it through the air with a quick snap of irritation.

The smile left Sebastian's mouth, and he licked his dry lower lip and stared at Farleigh with raw need.

"And don't you dare look at me like that! I should throw you into one of those stalls right this minute and fuck you blind, you beautiful man."

Sebastian shut his eyes and bit his lower lip. "How divine . . ."

Much closer to Sebastian, nearly kissing his ear, Farleigh whispered hoarsely, "Anna had better release you into my care when we arrive at Mandeville House, or I shan't be held responsible for my actions."

The clatter of the next stagecoach snapped them both out of the hot intimacy of their conversation. Farleigh called into the darkened stables. "Change out the horses, man. We'll be ready to leave immediately after lunch." With that, Farleigh turned toward the entrance of the inn and began walking across the stable yard. "Come, Sebastian. Anna and Pia will be here shortly, and I want to make good time this afternoon."

Sebastian followed him into the inn, where the two men were led to the private room the innkeeper had set up in anticipation of their arrival. A wide array of cold meats and fresh vegetables were neatly presented, and then the innkeeper left. The food remained untouched, Farleigh and Sebastian sitting silently at opposite ends of the table, until Pia and Anna came tumbling in, full of laughter and gaiety.

"What a splendid journey!" Anna crowed. "The English countryside is as refreshing and verdant as I'd always imagined." She must have sensed the tension in the room. And she obviously liked it. She smiled sweetly at Farleigh then lifted her lips to Sebastian's cheek. "My lord."

Both men had risen when the ladies entered. The next hour passed in tense silence interspersed with the occasional comment. Near the end of the meal, when Anna realized Sebastian had barely touched his food, she asked, "What is it, love?"

"Oh, I don't have much of an appetite."

"Of course you must eat, darling," Anna chastised. "You are going to need your strength for all of those country pursuits. Isn't that right, Your Grace?" She looked at Farleigh with wide, questioning eyes, then she had the impudence to give him a suggestive wink.

"Damn you, Anna." He threw down his napkin. "Apologies, Sebastian. For damning your wife, that is. I am going to ride ahead to Mandeville House to ensure everything is in order for your arrival. The drivers and footmen are well acquainted with the route. I beg you forgive me." With that, he bowed formally and left the room.

"Well, well, well." Anna popped a crisp radish into her mouth. After she finished chewing, she looked at Sebastian. "I think tomorrow's the day, don't you?"

Sebastian leapt from his chair and pulled her face between his hands, kissing her wildly.

"I love you," he said between kisses. Then he reached over to Pia and pulled her in for a kiss, as well. "I love you, too, sweet Pia. You and your inquisitive eyes have been driving me to distraction." He kissed her again, then whispered hotly, "I want to see your eyes aglow when Farleigh takes me."

Pia softened into him, a low moan escaping from deep in her throat. Anna let her fingertips trace the edge of Pia's bodice near her breast, driving all three of them into a frenzy. Sebastian's firm hand tightened at the back of Pia's neck. Anna was ready to order Sebastian to his knees, the anticipation of Farleigh entering their intimate world creating a hot wave of longing in all of them—

The door to the private eating chamber swung open and all three of them stumbled to their feet, standing up far too quickly to be graceful—moist-lipped, wide-eyed, and guilty as sin.

"Enough!" Farleigh cried. "Into the carriage. All of you." When none of them moved from their frozen spots, he practically bellowed, "Now!"

They swept past him and hustled out the front door of the Falcon, where Farleigh's carriage awaited with fresh horses. After both women were inside, Farleigh shut the door for a moment, holding on to the handle with a knuckle-whitening grip that prevented Sebastian from joining the ladies. Still, Anna could hear the conversation through the thin glass.

"So, I take it you no longer wish for me to ride with you on the rest of the journey to Mandeville House?" Sebastian asked.

"That is correct."

"Will you care to see me once we arrive?" Sebastian asked. Anna adored the sound of clamoring desperation that tinged his words.

Farleigh's voice took on a menacing tone, "Oh, I will care to *see* you, Sebastian. Naked and on your knees." Anna gasped as Farleigh pulled open the door with a violent tug. "Get in."

Sebastian quickly jumped up to join the ladies in the carriage. Farleigh slammed the door shut, quite nearly taking off Sebastian's foot at the ankle while he was at it.

Pia looked out the carriage as the tiny village of Gamlingay passed by. In some ways, it reminded her of Burgos. It was difficult to comprehend how much of her life—how many long years—had faded into a blink while the past month had erupted into a rich and varied tapestry that would stay with her for the rest of her life. It was high summer, and they had been on the road for many hours. Anna and Sebastian had fallen asleep shortly after they departed Stevenage, but she was too excited to be tired.

About fifteen minutes after they trotted through Gamlingay, the carriage turned between two grand columns and passed through a large wrought iron gate. A kindly looking older man waved his cap in welcome from where he stood on the low step in front of the gatehouse.

"Wake up, you two," Pia whispered, nudging each of their knees. "We are here."

Sebastian stirred first. His beautiful blue-green eyes looked glassy and youthful, opening slowly like a child's after a long snooze. He smiled at Pia then leaned down to kiss Anna awake. "We're here, darling."

Anna opened her eyes and stretched her slender arms above her head, then let out a big yawn. Within seconds she was fully awake. "How exciting!" She clapped her hands together, startling Pia and Sebastian. They all laughed, and a few minutes later they were pulling in front of the massive portico with its eight enormous columns and wide, shallow steps.

A dozen liveried servants were lined up, six on either side of the imposing front door, to assist with their arrival. There was no sign of Farleigh.

The three of them were escorted into the dining room where a splendid repast was waiting for them. Still, no sign of Farleigh.

Once they had eaten, sharing a bottle of extraordinary Spanish wine, they were shown to a large suite of three adjoining rooms. What had probably been designed as a guest suite for dignitaries who traveled with valet and lady's maid suited the three of them admirably. Their luggage had been unpacked and put away while they'd been down at supper. The butler asked if they were in need of any additional assistance.

Sebastian replied that they were very well situated, thank you. "But where is the master of the house?"

"His Grace sends his regrets. He was quite tired when he arrived and hopes you will excuse his absence this evening. He anticipates feeling better on the morrow and asks that you be ready to leave for a picnic at eleven."

"Thank you very much for all your kindness," Anna said.

The butler bowed and withdrew.

Once they were alone, Anna turned to Sebastian. "Farleigh's quite put out, isn't he?"

"Yes," Sebastian said, pulling her into his arms. "Quite."

She kissed him once, then patted him on the chest, over the lapel of his jacket. "Off you go."

"What?" he said with a smile of surprise.

"You, too, Pia." Anna gestured in the opposite direction. "I think we should all get a good night's sleep, don't you? Something tells me we're going to have a very busy day tomorrow."

Sebastian laughed out loud. "Oh, Anna. You are fabulous." He gave her one last kiss, quick and innocent on the lips, then reached for Pia and gave her a similar buss. "I love you both. I'll try to rest up for the big day, but I'm awfully excited."

"Well you'd better not do anything about it tonight."

"How do you mean?"

"No frigging," Anna chided. "Now, go to bed, Sebastian."

His eyes blinked slowly. "Yes, my love." He walked away, turning to blow each of them a kiss before entering the connecting room and pulling the door shut behind him.

"You, too, darling." Anna kissed Pia one last time. "I feel like I did the night before you and I first walked into the forest . . . I was so nervous and excited. I knew I had to tell you how I felt—even if you didn't share my feelings and it meant you would shun me. I am set to burst at the prospect of seeing Farleigh take Sebastian." She shivered.

"So am I." Pia's body quaked with an answering ripple of anticipation, and she reached up to feel the throbbing of her own pulse at the base of her neck.

"Ah. No touching yourself tonight, Pia."

"Anna!" She glared at her tormentor.

"What? I'm only making it better for you. Think how worked up you're going to be. The two of them, finally ripping each other to shreds, and Farleigh making—"

"Stop!" Pia pleaded. "I can't spend another moment picturing the two of them or I'll combust."

"Precisely. Tomorrow we combust. Give me one last kiss, then off to our separate beds we go."

Anna taunted her with one final caress, dipping her finger into the edge of Pia's bodice and teasing her nipple into hard awareness.

"Anna . . . please let me . . ."

"Off you go."

Pia eventually fell asleep, but only after a restless hour spent imagining Farleigh pacing around his ducal suite like a caged panther.

Chapter 27

"So this is your home, then?" Pia asked the next morning.

Farleigh looked startled when he turned to see her descending the staircase, probably fearing she was accompanied by Sebastian and Anna. Then he smiled, likely relieved she was alone. "I suppose."

"Why only suppose?" She stepped off the last tread and stood near him in the front hall.

Farleigh shrugged. "It still feels like my father's home, even though he's been dead these three years. I'm not sure how I will ever fill it. My life is in town. Gallivanting, as it were." He smiled again, but Pia saw something wary around his eyes.

"Ah, I see."

"You do? Please enlighten me."

"You are looking for home. For the contentment the idea inspires. Aren't we all?"

His face turned stormy. "If that shrew of a woman—whom you both adore for some reason I shall never comprehend—would release Sebastian into my keeping, I think I should be entirely content."

Pia shook her head. "You adore Anna, too. I know you do. She's only . . . impeding you at the moment, and you don't like it."

"That's a very temperate way of saying how I feel about the current situation."

"But you think if you and Sebastian were together, that you would be . . . content?"

He nodded with total certainty. "Absolutely. Seeing him again after these years apart has only fomented the feelings I had for him while we were together in Spain. Sebastian is . . . wonderful."

"I agree. I mean . . ." She blushed. "Of course, I agree."

"You still blush, Pia? After all the things . . ."

She raised a quizzical brow, looking at him boldly. "All what things, Farleigh?" Yes, she had done *all the things* with Anna and Sebastian, but it was so much more than that. They *were* her home—in their arms she felt the contentment and peace Farleigh alluded to.

When he did not answer her question, she stated coolly, "I fear you do not possess emotional gravity."

"Why?" He was angry now. "Because I have admitted to my gallivanting ways, to my wild youth, you think I am incapable of a deeper feeling? That's a hateful thing to say, Pia."

Good. She liked to see him angry like this. It meant he cared. On the outside, he was so immaculate. She looked at how his clothes were practically sewn on to his muscular frame; she let her eyes travel to his perfectly polished Hessian boots. But for Sebastian's sake—for all their sakes—she needed to see not only the physical lust which was practically emanating off him like sparks from a flint but the emotional depth, the desire for commitment over consummation, that would keep the four of them together for the rest of their lives.

"I meant it in a loving way," she said gently.

His pale eyes twinkled in the dim light of the large front hall where she had happened upon him. Sebastian and Anna were strolling in the gardens, killing time until eleven, when the four of them were set to meet. Or more to the point, when Sebastian was to be handed over to Farleigh.

"Such a shame you do not fancy a woman's touch," she said. Yes, he had joked of marrying her to fulfill his ducal duties, but she wanted, if not all of him—he would always adore Sebastian and that was fine with her—at least some small part that he could give of himself, that would be hers. Perhaps even a family, children. Her deeper interest probably shone bright in her gaze, but she couldn't—or didn't want to—conceal it.

"I'm not *entirely* opposed." He stared at her mouth and took a step closer to her. "I will have to learn to tolerate a woman's touch at one point or another. I have to beget an heir, after all. You'd do as well as any."

She smiled ruefully and took a step away from him. "You make it sound so thrilling, Farleigh."

He laughed. "Sorry. That's how it makes me feel. Since we're being honest."

"You remind me so much of Anna, so it's funny to hear you pretend to dislike her. It would be akin to disliking yourself."

"Sometimes I dislike myself," he tried.

"Very infrequently, I imagine!"

He smiled and held out his arm. "Come. I have something I've been looking forward to sharing with you." She rested her hand on his forearm, and he led her down the corridor. He stopped in front of a pair of wide oak doors, then opened them to reveal an enormous picture and sculpture gallery.

Pia gasped in pleasure. "Oh, how utterly divine!"

"I'm so glad you approve. I know how much you enjoy painting. Have you ever sculpted?"

"Yes. No." Pia covered her mouth, not wanting to gape, but it was impossible. "Yes, I have painted, but very infrequently. Canvas and oil were far too dear. For the most part, I sketched and drew with charcoal. And I've never sculpted. I've always wanted to. Oh, Farleigh, this is so fabulous. Where . . .? How . . .?" There were marbles and paintings, drawings and etchings. The walls were covered from the tilt of the tray ceiling to the baseboard molding near the wood floor.

"I enjoy collecting."

"So you do," Pia agreed. "May I?" she asked, reaching out to one of the classical Greek marbles.

"Absolutely. That's why I bought them. So they would be mine to do with as I wished." He watched her hand caress the turn of the goddess's breast, then across the slight roundness of her belly. Pia felt his eyes on her as she touched the cool mound at the apex of the statue's smooth thighs.

"She is so lovely," Pia whispered reverently. "Where did you get her?"

"I fancy her, too. I got her in Athens. She is my kind of woman. Serene. Contained. Strong."

The statue depicted Artemis, the huntress, and it was not lost on Pia that the powerful marble goddess held a striking resemblance to herself. She turned quickly to see Farleigh adjusting the cuff of his already perfect shirt. "Really?"

He shrugged again. "I like her. Aesthetically."

"So it's possible?"

He laughed again, low and self-assured. "I'm not repulsed by a woman's body, if that's what you're asking. It's . . . how to say it? The society we live in expects women to be dirty whores or wifely virgins. Neither of which appeals to me in the least. With men, I can be an animal."

Pia burst out laughing.

He smiled too and waited until she'd settled down to continue. "I meant, when I am with a man, I can be a human being—a human animal—in my natural state, not a gentleman with a lady or a customer with a prostitute."

"I think I would very much like to see you in your natural state."

He reached out and took her hand in his. "I think today might be our lucky day." He smiled again and led her over to a statue of a nude male Adonis. "I have a wonderful picnic planned."

"You do?" She squeezed his hand. "Pray tell."

"You'll see soon enough. Come. Look at my favorite statue." Perched on a low pediment, the sculpture was positioned so strong thighs and relaxed genitals were right at eye level. The Greek god's taut body was turned in preparation to throw the discus. Farleigh maneuvered himself so he stood behind Pia, then lifted her hand with his.

A thrilling heat spread across her back, where Farleigh's body pressed near, his chest and arms caging her in. She nearly melted at the prospect of being skin to skin in the same position, his hard, unforgiving flesh pressing against her sensitive back. "Ah," she murmured, pretending to pay attention to the statue.

He placed both of their hands along the marble thigh. "I love the strength of this muscle, the coiled power." His hand rose higher, keeping Pia's beneath his. Her breath became shallow. She was only a few inches shorter than he was, but she had to stretch onto her tiptoes to reach the side of Adonis's hip, where Farleigh stopped. "I love the turn of this arse," he whispered, hot and close to her ear.

Pia felt the press of Farleigh's cock against her lower back, the beginning of his physical arousal. *Probably from imagining what he would do with that arse.*

"I love the feel of being here between these two pillars of strength," Pia whispered. "I never would have imagined . . ." She leaned back into Farleigh. A few seconds later, the door opened and a flushed Anna and Sebastian strolled into the gallery.

"Ah! There you are," Sebastian said, smiling at the two of them caught in the act of caressing the naked statue.

Pia gasped. "We were just—"

Strangely, Farleigh pulled her tighter against him, maybe to conceal his erection, but it felt more possessive than that. Perhaps he wanted to hold her hostage until he could get a hold of Sebastian. Pia let him.

They all stared at one another, each of them weighing their own desires against the powerful desires of the other three people in the room. As the silence crackled between the four of them, Sebastian and Anna walked slowly across the gallery until they were standing side by side, mere inches in front of Pia.

"Hello, my love," Anna whispered and leaned up to kiss her full on the lips, so close to Farleigh, so close to Sebastian, all of them so close. Pia whimpered and kissed her back. God, how she loved this woman. Reaching her free hand into Anna's blonde hair, Pia felt Farleigh's hold tighten and remembered where she was. She pressed her bottom more firmly against him and felt the answering twitch of his cock. Anna slowed down the kiss but reached up to caress Pia's breast.

When Anna finished kissing her, Pia looked up to see Sebastian and Farleigh staring at one another with nothing short of tightly reined animal ferocity. "The picnic carriage is ready," Farleigh growled. "Let us be off." He released Pia and strode past Anna and Sebastian without looking back.

Chapter 28

The carriage was a glorious, open-air affair. Farleigh had spent a small fortune on it, but he had no regrets. He sat up in the high seat and the other three rode in the back. After about twenty minutes of trotting along a narrow grassy lane into a wooded part of the estate, they emerged into his favorite glade. He drew the horses to a halt and stepped off the high perch.

He handed the reins to one of the servants, who was there for that purpose. Another footman had also come to ensure all the food was properly iced and presented.

"We're here," Farleigh said to his guests. He reached up to help Pia step from the high carriage. Sebastian helped Anna.

"Will that be all, sir?" the footman asked.

"Yes. Please do not return with the carriage until tomorrow morning."

"Tomorrow morning?" Anna balked.

Farleigh's head turned slowly. "Yes, señora de Montizon. Tomorrow morning. Unless you'd prefer the comfort of your feather bed back at Mandeville House, in which case you may accompany these fine fellows." He gestured vaguely toward the two servants who were ready to leave. One of the men had mounted Farleigh's carriage and the other was getting ready to depart in the wagon that had been used to transport all the food and gear.

Anna's back stiffened. "No, thank you. I believe I'll stay."

Farleigh began to turn away.

"But twenty-four hours is very long for a picnic—" Anna started to quibble.

Farleigh, turning back with disciplined slowness, said, "It may not be long enough for what I have in mind. Are you sure you wish to remain?"

She smiled at last, and Farleigh finally began to suspect she was his ally, not his enemy. "I am quite sure, Your Grace. This is the privacy and solitude I have been hoping for all these long weeks. It will be quite lovely for the four of us to relax and become . . . familiar." In that moment, he could tell from that serene smile that all she had ever wanted was what was best for Sebastian—for all of them, really. "I'm quite fond of very long picnics. Pardon me for questioning your proposal." She curtsied politely and walked toward the small lake where Sebastian and Pia were already laughing and pointing out some beautiful plant or other.

Farleigh looked over all the arrangements, making sure the servants had done all he'd asked, then he gave them permission to leave. They had spent many hours this morning executing his orders: two white linen tents had been constructed. One was filled with iced delicacies—potted shrimp, oysters, cool wine—the other was a sybaritic pile of silk and satin pillows heaped atop a carpet of animal skins, with two trunks storing kimonos and sarongs and other delights from his travels in the West Indies and the Orient.

Needless to say, Farleigh would happily forgo the food.

He pulled off his confining jacket and tossed it over one of the canvas campaign chairs. Pulling off his boots and silk socks, he reveled in the feel of the cool grass between his toes. He watched as Anna and Pia laughed together by the lake, then he stared at the turn of Sebastian's shoulders, narrow hips, and backside. He must have felt the weight of Farleigh's attention because he turned and stared back. The two of them were held like that for a few seconds. Farleigh continued undressing. He planned on being unclothed for the rest of the day and night.

Sebastian's eyes on him turned the casual act of disrobing into something turbulent. He pulled his shirt over his head, then undid his buckskins, all while staring across the distance at Sebastian's partially opened mouth. When he was naked, finally, after all the weeks of torture, he strode toward the lake.

Anna and Pia were standing close to one another, their hands gripped together. "Oh," Pia whispered when he passed.

He dove into the lake and swam out to the center without saying a word to any of them. When he came up for air, he burst out laughing. All three of them were scrambling to get their clothes off as quickly as they could. He called out, "Are you finally in a rush, Anna?"

"I am!" she called back. She was helping Pia undo her corset, while a perfectly nude Sebastian helped Anna remove hers. Farleigh was treading water so his heart rate was already accelerated, but seeing the three of them like that made his heart constrict and pound harder. He wanted to be part of that, to be joined the way they were. Not only for the sensual pleasures but for the daily intimacy of touch and caring.

After having spent his whole life believing adulthood required that he divide duty from desire, Farleigh was chilled and breathless when he glimpsed the potential future that was standing right before him. The water was cold against his skin but the chill came from the terrifying hope that he could be joined with these three people, that the four of them—together—could define and direct their lives as they wished. The terror came from the same sliver of fear that had always dogged him: that he didn't deserve that kind of fulfillment, that a consuming happiness was reserved for *good* people. And he had been led to believe—by society and its self-appointed judges—that his particular desires made him a very bad person.

He watched as Sebastian finished helping the women, then dove into the lake. A few seconds later, his slick face popped up a few feet away, like an otter.

"Farleigh . . ." Sebastian swam up to him and wrapped his arms around his neck and coiled his strong legs around Farleigh's hips. "Kiss me, man."

Farleigh would not have called what followed a kiss—more of a ravishment. He pulled at Sebastian's wet hair, tugging and scratching him, the two of them like a pair of sea creatures set free at last. Eventually, after they became winded, Farleigh pulled them to shore, desperate to see all of Sebastian while he touched him and made Sebastian's body bend to his will.

"God, how desperate I am for you," Sebastian gasped as Farleigh slammed him to the soft, earthy edge of the lake. They lay side by side, panting and staring at the crystalline blue sky.

"What shall we do about it?" Farleigh teased.

Sebastian turned on his side and rested his head on his palm, staring down the length of Farleigh's body. Farleigh watched out of the corner of his eye as Sebastian licked his lips and looked down at

Farleigh's jutting cock. "Come, Seb. Suck me off quickly, for a start, to sand off this jagged edge." Farleigh spread his strong thighs, letting his legs rest wide and inviting.

Sebastian sat up and shifted so he was on his bent knees, crouched near Farleigh's cock. "How do you want it?" Sebastian asked.

"Hard and fast."

Before he'd finished the three short words, Sebastian had pulled him into his mouth with enough force to knock the breath out of both of them. When Farleigh recovered enough to realize he was finally getting what he'd been anticipating every minute of the past few weeks, he let out a satisfied groan.

Sebastian made a similar noise, the vibration at the back of his throat shooting up Farleigh's spine.

Lifting himself up on his elbows, Farleigh watched Sebastian's incredible mouth, the strain of his lips, the tension of his cheeks. "God, you are so miraculous, Seb."

Sebastian's eyes—at half-mast while he worked—closed in pleasure at Farleigh's praise. The force of his powerful mouth paired with the sweet gentleness of those thick black eyelashes put Farleigh right over. He cried out his release within minutes, slamming his hips up into Sebastian's face and loving the way Sebastian sucked harder still, wanting every drop of him. So beautifully desperate.

When Sebastian flopped back onto the moist earth, Farleigh said, "Come here, boy." He reached out one arm and pulled Sebastian into his hold, so his dark hair, still wet from their swim, was cool against his pounding chest. "Jesus, Sebastian. I've wanted you terribly."

Sebastian was slowly rocking his cock against Farleigh's hip and humming his pleasure at being in the man's arms. "And I you."

They stayed like that, with their eyes closed and the summer air caressing their bare skin, listening to the noises of the forest and the animals around the lake mix with the laughter and tender sounds of Anna and Pia swimming nearby in the shallows.

Waking about half an hour later, Farleigh opened his eyes to see Anna in one of his rich brocade caftans. She was reclining against a tree a few feet away, reading aloud from a book while she caressed Pia's cheek. Pia smiled when he caught her eye, her head on Anna's lap. He was able to decipher a few scraps of what Anna was reading and realized they must have raided his trunks and were enjoying one of the erotic novels he'd found on his travels.

He smiled back at Pia then glanced at her lush body; she looked so completely at ease with her naked flesh against the grass, almost as if she had risen up out of the earth like a mythological creature. Sebastian rustled in his arms and came slowly awake. Gorgeously aroused.

Rested and ready, thought Farleigh with a sharp spike of desire.

Pia gazed up to see Anna had fallen quiet, her attention on the two men. Pia watched as Anna's face turned from scientific wonder to elemental lust.

"Oh my," Anna whispered.

Pia turned to see Sebastian's head pulled back at a seemingly painful angle, with Farleigh tugging on his hair and making ravenous love to his mouth while pinning him down with one strong thigh across his hips. The duke was somehow beautifully loving and brutally demanding at the same time, making Sebastian appear almost weak by comparison.

But he wasn't weak. Sebastian was terribly strong, as both Anna and Pia knew firsthand. When Pia looked closer, she realized that Sebastian was actually resisting, his strength forcing both men to strain all of their muscles in order to hold each other in that intense grip.

Farleigh pulled his lips away from Sebastian. "God, you are splendid."

Sebastian looked so blissfully happy, his neck muscles straining, his mouth open. So open. *Open to anything*, Pia thought with a lustful sigh.

"Oh my," Pia echoed. "Should we leave them to it? It's almost too much."

Anna was silent, her eyes wide, darting from Sebastian's mouth—wet and open—to Farleigh's mouth, closed and showing the hint of a deviant smile.

"I think I want to fuck you properly while your two women watch. Would you like that, Sebastian?"

Pia covered her mouth again, appalled and delighted. Anna was simply delighted.

"Into the larger tent," Farleigh ordered as he stared into Sebastian's glowing dark eyes. "One and all."

Farleigh released Sebastian's hair after one last rough tug then pulled him quickly to his feet and into a one-armed hold. "This way, you beautiful man." The two of them sauntered toward the tent until Farleigh turned his head at the last minute and called lightly, "Are you joining us, ladies?"

He might as well have been inviting them to tea, the way he tossed the words over his shoulder like an afterthought. Anna grabbed Pia's hand, and both women leapt up and trotted quickly behind the men as they took long strides toward the sinful harem-like den Farleigh had created.

Chapter 29

Sebastian had always adored Farleigh's combination of devil-may-care and blinding intensity. As a political attaché in Spain, Farleigh had been dedicated and responsible, but away from those obligations he was bold and daring. So much like Anna in some ways—or what Anna would have been like if she had been raised in a world of power and privilege as Farleigh had been. Sebastian shivered at the prospect of how glorious Anna would be—was already becoming—in full possession of her sexual power, as well as the power to command everything a large purse could provide.

Soon enough.

"Taking a chill?" Farleigh asked.

Sebastian smiled at him. "Not in the least. I was thinking how much you remind me of my wife."

Farleigh laughed aloud and turned to look at the two women close on their heels. "That little sprite of a thing?"

"I wouldn't underestimate her. She is quite . . . ambitious."

Shaking his head, Farleigh said, "I think I can handle myself . . . and you for that matter." In a lower voice, he continued, "How rough can I be? I don't want to frighten the ladies, but I've missed you."

"Do with me what you will. Anna has given her blessing." He paused for a moment to look over his shoulder. "And I think Pia is in a state of lust-induced shock. She'd probably marry you after all, if you asked her."

Pursing his lips at the possibility, Farleigh said, "Mightn't be a bad solution, you know?"

"I was not being serious. Are you daft?"

Farleigh raised an eyebrow as he pulled back the curtain to the tent. "It would bind us to one another in a way society would never allow otherwise. We could be together."

Sebastian realized Pia and Anna were standing close and had heard what Farleigh had said. He looked at Anna and Pia and saw the tenderness and joy he always did, but there was something more: he felt as if the four of them made up a solid unit, a perfectly balanced whole.

"We could live openly as two couples. You and Anna, obviously." Farleigh looked at Pia. "Perhaps Pia could come to tolerate me." He reached out and touched her moist bottom lip.

He pulled his hand away slowly, and Pia gasped, then said, "I think that would be the most wonderful life I could ever dream of." She looked at Anna. "With all of us, together?"

Anna leaned in and kissed her passionately. Without another thought, Sebastian turned to Farleigh and the two of them slammed into another open-mouthed, fiery kiss.

When they finally pulled apart, Farleigh stared at Sebastian's mouth, then slowly shifted his gaze to look at Pia. "May I?"

Sebastian watched Pia realize Farleigh was asking if he could kiss her, that he was proposing to her in some elemental way. She nodded gently, and he dipped his head down to touch her mouth with his.

He was far more timid than he had been with Sebastian. Pia scowled. "If you plan on kissing me like some delicate flower, you'd best not kiss me at all."

Sebastian laughed when Farleigh slammed his mouth against hers and grabbed her bare breast with rough possession. She obviously loved the raw, demanding nature of Farleigh's lovemaking as she arched into his hold and widened her mouth for his penetrating assault.

As they finally pulled away from one another, panting and staring wildly at the unexpected lust in each other's eyes, Sebastian watched Anna closely.

"I thought I would be so afraid of losing you, Pia," Anna said quietly, "but this is what we've always wanted, isn't it? To be together?"

Pia's eyes were wide. "It's beyond anything I could have imagined. To have so much love." Anna leaned toward her and kissed her, softly at first, then biting Pia's lip the way she adored.

Anna turned to Farleigh. "She likes that."

He rolled his eyes. "I think I'll be able to sort out what she likes, Anna."

Sebastian laughed at what he now saw was going to be a glorious lifetime of openness and joy between the four of them. The banter and honesty of a true family, he thought, rather than the formal strictures under which each of them had been raised.

Opening the draped door to the tent wider, Sebastian gestured for the other three to enter. "Let us go in. Shall we?"

The diffused afternoon sunlight created a golden aura around their strong naked bodies and illuminated the fabrics, carpets, and unlit candles that had been spread everywhere. Farleigh came in last. "Well, here we all are," he began.

Sebastian felt the man's voice travel down his spine and looked at Anna and Pia to share his excitement. They both smiled at him, and he nodded.

"Let me take a good look at you, Sebastian. Kneel down," Farleigh ordered, leaning casually against one of the posts of the tent.

He knelt slowly, then clasped his hands behind his neck.

"Ah, yes, you remember. Very nice, Sebastian," Farleigh said in a low, approving voice. Sebastian's stiff cock twitched under the other man's admiration. "And look at you, always at the ready."

The afternoon air mingled with the sounds of summer leaves and a few birds. It was as if nature, in all of its miraculous variety, wafted around them and through them, touching their skin and declaring them part of the universe.

Sebastian began to feel the warmth of his submission thrum through his veins. He'd been with each of them in turn, and Pia and Anna together, but Farleigh's presence brought everything into such a strange and wonderful alignment. Of course, he had wondered whether or not his British friend would still be keen to pursue their lively physical relationship, but it was not the type of thing one mentioned in written correspondence about lodging in Mayfair and spending the Season with a duke.

Do you still fancy a right good rogering, then?

But when they had arrived and he'd realized how badly Farleigh wanted him, everything had changed. Anna had turned their mutual attraction into this powerful, desperate thing by forcing them to postpone it. Now Farleigh was implying they might all four be together in the future, forever, that such a thing was even possible.

"He's even more beautiful than my statue, isn't he, Pia?"

"Yes, Your Grace. He is." Pia gasped as Anna leaned in and kissed her neck and then further down, sucking on the tips of her breasts. "Keep looking at them," Anna whispered to Pia, but the tent was so quiet Sebastian could feel his wife's hushed words like licks on his backside.

Stepping quietly across the soft bearskin rug, Farleigh began to circle Sebastian's naked body. Examining. Appreciating. Contemplating. "Whatever am I going to do with you? So many magnificent possibilities."

Sebastian felt every inch of his skin becoming more and more sensitized. A light touch was going to scorch. Something harsher would bring him far greater pleasure. Pia was moaning softly as Anna began to fondle her between her legs with knowing fingers, her mouth never leaving Pia's bare breasts. Sebastian wanted to be consumed and released into the world of intense ecstasy that Farleigh's whip could provide.

As if reading his mind, Farleigh turned to open one of the smaller trunks. "Crop . . . short whip . . . the cat . . ." Farleigh tapped his lip while he contemplated his options.

Sebastian began to shake with desire—watching the pull and strain of Farleigh's taut muscles as he bent over the trunk—and then forced himself to breathe through his anticipation.

Farleigh chose a short whip and crossed back to the center of the room to show it to Sebastian. Dragging the flexible tip lightly along his jaw, across his forehead, then letting it hover tantalizingly close to his full lips, Farleigh finally asked, "Is this what you want?" Farleigh held it perfectly still until Sebastian bent to place his lips on the fine leather. He let his tongue slip around the braided texture of the narrow handle, knowing it would taste and smell like Farleigh's sweaty hand.

Pia cried out and Sebastian glanced quickly to see Anna's lips circling her nipple in much the same way his were circling the leather. When Sebastian returned his gaze to Farleigh's face, the duke was looking at Pia's wide, glistening eyes and smiling.

"You like that, Pia?"

"I do," she whispered. "Very much."

Then, with feigned impatience, he turned back to Sebastian. "No showing off," the duke bit out, withdrawing the handle immediately.

"Yes, sir," Sebastian replied, slipping easily and gratefully into the world of exquisite submissive pleasure.

Chapter 30

Anna watched as Farleigh expertly swatted the whip against Sebastian's perfectly turned arse and strong thighs. Sebastian's slightly opened lips and closed eyes were a sight to behold. He was an angel, with his hands clasped behind his neck and his arms bent like wings. The pose strained Sebastian's upper arms delightfully and dipped his lower back into a perfect arc.

Every time the whip slapped against Sebastian's skin, Anna looked at how the rest of his body rode the initial sting of pain and quickly transformed it into hot, liquid pleasure. She would demand instruction from Farleigh on that particular tool. It was longer than her crop and had a tapering length of hide at the end, like a short drafting whip, rather than the rounded, fold-over tip to which she had become accustomed. Farleigh had a militaristic precision that brought the most superb red stripes to the surface of Sebastian's immaculate flesh. They were nothing like the small square patterns she loved making with the riding crop; the whip left long, even welts across Sebastian's skin. The marks looked serious—lasting—as if Farleigh were branding him. Ever since Farleigh had kissed Pia at the entrance to the tent, the entire scene had taken on a weighty permanence, as if all four of them were building the foundation of their future together.

Meanwhile, Anna's hands roamed Pia's full breasts, squeezing and kneading, torturing her in that absentminded way Pia adored. Pia squirmed and begged next to her on the lush pillows, like the sweet thing she was. Momentarily turning her eyes away from the glorious spectacle of Farleigh whipping Sebastian into a frenzy of lust, Anna bit Pia's earlobe and commanded, "Stand up, darling, I want Farleigh to see you come."

Pia groaned and complied immediately, stretching to her full height, extending her arms up until she could nearly touch the fabric at the ceiling, then letting them rest near the tops of her long, muscled legs.

Farleigh paused for a moment to look at her. "My ... You are quite something, aren't you, Patrizia ..."

Pia stared at him boldly and sniped, "I thought you did not fancy women?"

He swatted the whip through the air with an impatient, repetitive motion. Sebastian seemed to respond as if the quick lashes were connecting with his own skin. Anna felt as though the room were contracting and expanding around her. When she let herself be free of her preconceptions—of her small-minded possessiveness—the possibilities among the four of them were truly endless.

Anna stood up and walked toward Farleigh, the large caftan swishing around her like a gust of powerful wind. His eyes narrowed as if he were about to be challenged.

"I believe Pia just disrespected you, and she is in need of punishment."

"Anna! No!" Pia cried.

Farleigh smiled. "I think you are quite right, my lady." He looked over at Pia meaningfully, then back at Anna. "But what about poor Sebastian? He has been so good and deserves his reward."

Anna began dragging her nails through Sebastian's sweaty hair. "He is so good, is he not? May I keep him warm for you while you see to Pia?"

Sebastian released a sigh of pleasure.

"Excellent idea." Farleigh offered her the whip handle.

"Actually," she said as she walked toward the open trunk that kept the leather items, "I fancy a turn at this suede flogger. I've never had the opportunity. Would you mind?"

Farleigh smiled again when he saw Sebastian's muscles clench and quiver in anticipation. "*Mind?*" He laughed. "Of course not. Have you ever used it on him before? It's one of his favorites, if I recall correctly. Isn't it, Seb?"

"Yes, sir."

Anna loved how Sebastian's voice had dropped to an even deeper register. He sounded so rutty and wild. She trailed the velvety leather strips along his bunched shoulders and down his spine. It wasn't as cruel as the cat-o'-nine-tails she'd seen on board the ship they'd taken from Bilbao, which had those menacing knots at the end of each strip. This was going to provide a much softer assault.

"Have you ever used it, Anna?" Farleigh asked.

"No." Anna fondled the baby-soft suede of the strands as she answered him.

"It is quite a delicate art. Let me show you." He held his hand over hers and gave a few twitches. "Like a whisk. Do you feel it?" She nodded. "Start lightly and you'll see the color begin to rise to the surface of his skin. Momentum is key. I suspect you'll both enjoy lots and lots of practice." Anna smiled at her new ally. "But I must attend to Pia, it seems. What would you like me to do to her?" Pia gasped, and Anna smiled. Farleigh might be her new best friend.

"A good old-fashioned spanking, if you will." Anna lifted one small hand. "I've never been able to give her what she properly deserves in that department. I'm simply not built for it."

"Allow me." He pivoted on his heel and grabbed Pia as she tried to dart out of reach.

"Anna!" she called, but Anna and Pia had negotiated secret words and gestures long ago that would put a stop to their more ambitious play.

"You know the words to say if you want him to stop, my darling. And *Anna* is not one of them."

Pia groaned, the sound a mixture of trepidation and joy. Farleigh pulled them both onto a pile of pillows and positioned her abdomen across his lap.

"Ready when you are, Lady Anna." Farleigh waited with one hand slightly raised while Anna whipped the flogger through the air, measuring its heft and power while those vibrating, singing breaths of empty air caused a thrilling response in Sebastian. She watched the way his back muscles bunched and relaxed, and listened to the way his breathing stuttered into a moan of anticipation.

"I believe we're ready, Your Grace."

And then they began. Anna started with a succession of light swats across Sebastian's hard thighs and buttocks while Farleigh made Pia count off spank after spank. Anna's wrist movements and rhythm had improved considerably since her wedding night, and her control of the flogger was fluid and sure after a few strokes. Sebastian arched his back in the most glorious pleasure as she used the long soft-sueded strips to warm and tighten his skin. She avoided the welts that Farleigh had created, suspecting the intensity might cause Sebastian to lose consciousness.

Meanwhile, the sound of Pia's desperation reverberated through Anna's core. Pia's keening, pleading, guttural responses to Farleigh's relentless strokes against her bottom were apparently making all of them that much more aroused. She watched as Sebastian's body rode the waves of pain and pleasure, processed the sounds of Pia's cries and Farleigh's smacks, and even Anna's own labored breathing.

Her rhythm with the flogger became perfectly synchronous with Farleigh's rhythm against Pia. It was akin to a musical performance, weaving in rests and peaks, fashioning the different notes of desire and agony into a shared symphony.

"Anna . . ." Sebastian whispered.

"What is it, love?" She'd pulled the flogger away from him and leaned down to breathe the words into his ear. While she dragged the very tips of suede along his tender skin, letting the leather kiss his flesh, she looked over to see if Farleigh was likewise finished. He nodded his agreement and turned the weeping Pia into his strong arms, cradling her and soothing her with words of praise and admiration.

Anna turned her full attention back to Sebastian, giving him a long lick up his neck to just below his ear, where she knew he was the most sensitive. He shivered and moaned, probably past any verbal reasoning. She kissed him one last time on the cheek, then circled around him, dragging the flogger along his cock and then up his muscled stomach and across the hard tips of his nipples.

Of all the things that had been done to him, she was surprised that the slight whispering caress of the suede against his chest was what finally made him cry out. That tiny, tender thing.

"Anna!" His eyes—dark and wild with passion—bored into hers while his hard cock jutted out from his body. "Anna," he repeated, almost a prayer this time.

"I love you, Sebastian," she whispered back.

Anna looked up again and realized it wasn't merely Sebastian who had soared into those misty corridors of ecstasy. All four of them had entered a shared realm of sweat and intense pleasure—Farleigh and Anna from the exertion and Pia and Sebastian from the endurance of it.

Anna dropped the flogger.

Breathing hard, she kissed Sebastian lightly on the neck. "Beautifully done, my darling," she praised. He shivered in response, his muscles straining from having held the position for so long. "Come." She helped him up and brought him to the silk-covered pile of pillows next to Farleigh and Pia. She arranged them so he could settle onto his stomach, ostensibly as a nod to his comfort, but in fact, so she could look her fill at his glorious, hot skin.

Anna watched as Farleigh continued to soothe Pia—who had wept delicious tears all during her thorough spanking and was now clinging to him fiercely, as if he were her savior rather than her tormentor. Anna trailed her fingernails lightly across Sebastian's gorgeously red arse and back. He quivered again, but he was past the ability to say any actual words. The lines Farleigh had created were miraculous. Anna traced them lovingly and relished Sebastian's answering moans of pleasure.

"These will not be gone anytime soon, my love. Such a beautiful memory for you." She leaned down and licked the length of one particularly vibrant welt. Sebastian whimpered into the turquoise satin pillow and relaxed deeper into her care.

Continuing to hold Pia close, Farleigh reached over to pick something up off a low table near where he was sprawled. He said something soothing and kind to Pia, then handed Anna an amber glass pot of salve. "Here," he whispered. "This will ensure he is comfortable." Anna opened it and smelled the exotic herbal fragrance, then rubbed it lovingly into Sebastian's skin.

After she finished tending to Sebastian, Anna turned to Farleigh. "May I have a word?"

He kept rocking Pia, smoothing her hair and kissing her tenderly, comforting her in much the same way Anna had cared for Sebastian. When he looked as though he was finally satisfied that she was properly soothed, Farleigh looked up and nodded as he set Pia gently on the makeshift bed alongside Sebastian, also on her stomach with her bright-red arse tilted similarly upward.

Anna felt hot all over. She wanted everything all at once. Sebastian's cock. Pia's mouth. Maybe even Farleigh's strong hands on her breasts. But first she wanted to see Farleigh take Sebastian, rough and hard and sure.

He joined her near the lightly blowing linen that served as the door, and she spoke quietly. "I suspect you are far more experienced than I am in this sort of thing."

He quirked his lips.

"As much as it pains me to admit it," she added quickly.

"Thought so," he said, crossing his arms in front of his large, muscled chest.

"But I am not stupid. Like a kitchen, too many chefs spoil the pot. Why don't we make this first time your turn to cook?"

"You will submit to me?" he asked with raised eyebrows.

"Don't be ridiculous," she whispered hoarsely. "Of course I shan't submit to you, but if you were inclined to orchestrate the proceedings in a way that allowed all of us to take our pleasure, I would be amenable."

He smiled. "I was only checking. I've no interest in breaking someone from her true nature . . . *Chef.* I like it. Let me think." He looked over his shoulder at the two beautiful languorous bodies, then back into Anna's eyes. "Are you willing to let me take Sebastian while you and Pia hold him down?"

Anna's face must have flushed at the prospect.

He laughed low and strong. "I'll take that as a most definitive yes." He finished describing what he had in mind, and Anna nodded here and there to let him know she was willing. She admired his creativity and made a mental note to allow herself the same freedom to imagine and improvise in the future. Oh, the mere idea! *The future.*

A few minutes later, Farleigh and Anna approached their lovers. Seb and Pia were holding hands and breathing deeply, not quite asleep, not quite awake. Farleigh leaned down to whisper so both Sebastian and Pia could hear. "Now for your just rewards. This afternoon, Anna and I decided, we are going to let Sebastian be the center of attention."

Chapter 31

Sebastian opened one eye and looked at Anna. She nodded and smiled, and he gave her a dreamy, acquiescent smile in return. He blinked slowly, trying to get his bearings, but he suspected he would be unmoored for the rest of his life.

He watched as Anna kissed Pia on the lips. "Wake up, my darling. I need you." Anna helped Pia stand up, then Anna held her arms wide as if Pia were her maid. Pia lovingly removed Anna's caftan and let it fall to the ground.

Sebastian sighed when Farleigh began kissing him more fully awake, nipping at his lips. "On your back, man." Sebastian obeyed, turning over to face them—Farleigh to his left, Anna and Pia to his right.

"How did I get so lucky?" Sebastian asked.

Anna leaned down. "Because you have been a very, very good boy." She tapped him playfully on the nose. "Now, keep in mind, Farleigh is in charge, but I still get to tell you when you can come. Inside me, all right?"

He reached for her cheek and touched her. "Yes, darling," he said as she took his hand and sucked his fingers into her mouth.

Farleigh took Sebastian's other hand and tied it firmly to one of the tent posts, then walked around to his other side and took Sebastian's hand from Anna's mouth and tied it to another post. Sebastian tested the resistance, then gave himself over completely to the feeling of utter freedom that he always felt when he was restrained. His bonds released him.

"There we are," Farleigh said, testing the tension one last time. "Now, Pia." Farleigh let his palm rest on her still-warm arse as he spoke to her. "You and Anna are going to need to keep Sebastian very open for me. Can you do that?"

Pia nodded, eyes wide.

"Very good."

Sebastian tilted his head back and thrust his cock into the air, moaning in anticipation.

"Not to worry, Sebastian. Anna is going to take care of your cock and Pia is going to take care of your mouth. You know where I'll be." Farleigh laughed low and opened another trunk. He moved a few things around then took out another porcelain jar and undid the lid.

"Anna and Pia, pull his knees back for me, will you?"

Sebastian groaned again when each woman climbed onto the bed of cushions on either side of him and did Farleigh's bidding while the duke walked slowly toward them.

"Oh yes." Farleigh dipped two fingers into the jar of ointment and set the container on the floor. Kneeling between Sebastian's spread legs, Farleigh began rubbing the lubricant all around Sebastian's quivering arsehole. "That's it. You're already opening for me, aren't you, Seb? Grabbing even."

"Yes. God, yes," he panted.

"I found this cream in a shop in the Caribbean, Seb. I thought you'd appreciate it." Anna and Pia watched as Farleigh inserted one, then two fingers deep into Sebastian. He writhed in delight, his eyes rolling to the back of his head as he was lost in the crushing wave of pleasure. His last barely coherent thought was gratitude for the bondage at his wrists that would assure his body remained safely tethered to the earth while his spirit soared in ecstasy.

Pia was torn; she didn't know whether to watch Farleigh's hand or Anna's beautiful face, slack with open-mouthed desire. Anna loved penetrating Sebastian—she had done so in Pia's presence any number of times, with any number of objects—but this afternoon was profoundly different. Pia thought Anna looked awestruck, as if by observing Farleigh—as he transformed Sebastian into something pliant and beautiful—Anna was finally able to appreciate the depth of her feelings for Sebastian.

Pia, on the other hand, was dreaming of a time when Farleigh would penetrate her in that way, so methodical, so confident.

"You like that, Pia." Farleigh caught her eye and drew her to him with nothing more than a glance. "Would you let me finger your arse like this?" Farleigh stared at Pia's hardening nipples as he kept up the ruthless momentum in and out of Sebastian.

"Oh God!" Sebastian cried out.

Pia moaned in sympathetic longing.

"That's only two fingers, my dear boy. I know you can take far more." With that, Anna and Pia watched—amazed—as a third finger joined the other two in that maddeningly slow in-and-out motion.

Once he had Sebastian writhing, screaming for more, Farleigh slowly removed his fingers. "Get me ready, Pia, while Anna soothes Sebastian for a moment."

Pia was stunned, unsure of what to do, so she looked to Anna. Reaching for her cheek, Anna caressed her lightly, then nodded and smiled her agreement. Pia melted into her touch, kissed her palm, then nearly dove at Farleigh's gorgeous cock. She licked her lips and knelt down to take him. It was wider than Sebastian's, and she reveled in the straining pull of her lips when she took him fully into the back of her throat.

She reveled, too, in his guttural moan of satisfaction and the harsh tug when his hand coiled into her long hair, guiding her rhythm. Anna was nearby, their heads only a few inches apart, while she was taking Sebastian in the same way. Anna's breathy moans accelerated Pia's lust.

Sebastian cried out again, his voice a slurring bliss of ecstasy.

Pia was lost in the carnal pleasure of having Farleigh, but she also craved Anna's hands on her. As if she sensed her need, Anna reached for Pia's sensitive breasts and began fondling her while they sucked off the men.

Farleigh's voice was an unfamiliar growl. "Now," he ordered. He pushed Pia's mouth away, and she was momentarily distraught that she hadn't pleased him. But when she stood up and looked in his eyes, she saw blissful satisfaction. "That was lovely, Pia . . ." His voice trailed off as he leaned in to kiss her, moaning into the taste of himself when his tongue swept into her mouth.

She reached for his strong arms, unsure of where or how to hold on to him. His strength was intoxicating, and she wanted to feel him against her, in her.

"Come here, darling," Anna said gently, guiding Pia away from Farleigh. Anna kissed her on the cheek. "You will have him again, sweetling. He adores you."

Pia looked over her shoulder at Farleigh and licked her lips again. "I adore him." While she said the words to Anna, it was Farleigh's eyes she held. Pia felt fearless, bold. She wanted him to know her feelings, how she had come to admire him, to yearn for him.

Anna kissed her again. "I know you do, my sweet. We all do. Now be a lamb and settle yourself over Sebastian's face, so he can taste you, but turn this way so I can kiss you while I fuck him."

Sebastian moaned in anticipation of the fresh onslaught. Pia straddled his chest, with her spread legs cradling his face. He angled his neck up to taste her, and Pia's head fell forward in ecstasy, her palms resting on his firm abdomen to keep her balance.

"Yes, darlings, that's lovely," Anna said, standing by the side of the bed and adjusting their positions slightly until everything was apparently to her liking. Pia felt Anna's fingers tracing Sebastian's lips where he was kissing Pia's pussy, then trailing her finger up and around Pia's puckering arse. "So lovely," Anna praised. Pia was already getting close to her release, and Anna must have sensed it. "Have a care you two," Anna warned, "we've still a ways to go."

They both moaned, Pia having leaned forward to take Sebastian's cock into her mouth.

"Yes, sweet Pia. Now you can watch Farleigh enter Sebastian."

Pia nearly cried with the pleasure of it, the overwhelming saturation of all of her senses carrying her nearly out of her body: the taste of Sebastian, the sight of Farleigh, the feel of Anna's light, encouraging caresses along her back.

"Is everything in order, Farleigh?" Anna asked, as if she were his aide-de-camp.

"Perfect," he replied with an answering smile. Pia watched as, inches from her face, Farleigh's strong hands spread Sebastian's thighs even wider before he settled his knees beneath him. Pausing to take one last breath, Farleigh then slowly pushed his huge cock into Sebastian's slick, tight hole.

Pia now knew why Farleigh had tied Sebastian's wrists. As she sucked him off and Farleigh penetrated him, the sweet man was beside himself. Thrashing and tugging at his restraints, head thrown back, he thrust up into Pia's mouth and then down onto Farleigh.

"Lovely," Anna whispered, pulling Sebastian's balls aside to get a better look at Farleigh's rhythm. Pia's face was right there, as Anna took a few more seconds to watch Farleigh's magnificent cock stretching Sebastian to the reaches of what he could endure.

Sebastian moaned again, nearing desperation. His vibrating mouth against her swollen sex sent sparks straight up Pia's spine, shooting hot prickles of sensation across her tender arse and bare back.

Anna squeezed his sac affectionately then let go. "Here I am, my love." She turned back and slowly lifted Pia's mouth from Sebastian's rod. She kissed Pia tenderly. "I love you, Pia," Anna whispered. "Arch up for me."

Pia lifted her eyes and saw Farleigh gazing at her while he kept up that slow, powerful pace in and out of Sebastian. Pia concentrated on Farleigh's eyes to keep the trembling onslaught of her orgasm from crashing over her as Sebastian's mouth worked her feverishly. While Anna circled behind him, Farleigh leaned down and kissed Pia's lips while he was fucking Sebastian, while Sebastian was licking her. The whip of pleasure cracked through her like thunder; she felt as though she might die from the simultaneous, overpowering love of both of these men at once. She swiveled her hips, riding hard against Sebastian's frantic mouth; she bit Farleigh's lip and battled her tongue against his. Both of them were entirely too much, but she couldn't get enough of either of them.

Farleigh pulled back from her mouth for a second, breathless. All four of them were frozen in that moment.

"Marry me, Pia."

Pia looked quickly from Farleigh's swollen lips to his eyes. "Yes," she whispered.

Anna clapped her hands in joy and then leaned down to kiss Pia. "Congratulations, darling." She looked from Pia to Farleigh and back again. "I hate to cut in." She winked and slid one leg languidly over Sebastian's hips. Pia watched as Anna rubbed the tip of his cock against her swollen clit. "Oh God, that's good," Anna whispered.

Sebastian begged for Anna to take him, having momentarily abandoned his attention to Pia's sex to gasp for air and cry out nearly incomprehensible phrases and supplications. Pia moaned in sympathetic longing as she watched Anna squeeze his cock and guide him into her. Sebastian began licking Pia again, and she cried out as he moaned into her sensitive flesh. He seemed to be lost in the exquisite triumvirate of pleasure: slamming up into Anna's pussy, or down onto Farleigh's cock, or lavishing his attention on Pia with his mouth.

"Come here, Pia," Anna whispered. "Put your fingers on my cunny, so you can feel when Sebastian comes."

Pia obeyed. She loved when Anna cried out as her deft fingers pleasured Anna in that familiar way, while Sebastian's cock thrust into Anna and Farleigh's cock thrust into Sebastian.

Soon, Pia's movements became disjointed and desperate, her tilted arse quivering in the moments before a release that would no longer be contained.

Sebastian pulled his mouth away from Pia and began tearing wildly at his restraints. He cried out Anna's name, then Farleigh's, then Pia's, all of them whipped together in a frenzy of ecstasy.

And then it wasn't frenetic at all. It was a beautiful dance, a ballet in which all four of them were one. Anna leaned her head back and arched against Farleigh's shoulder, then reached forward to fork her fingers through Pia's long black hair. Pia's hands, desperate and needy, worked on Anna's breasts, caressed her stomach, reached for her hips.

Sebastian bucked up into Anna with wild thrusts. Farleigh added something elemental, something that lent balance and power to all of them. He grunted and pushed into Sebastian with a roughness that Sebastian obviously found deeply satisfying from the sound of his low moans, and then Farleigh reached around Anna's body to hold Pia's hair, as well.

Sebastian's desperation finally reached such a pitch that even Anna looked like she might take mercy on him. "A moment longer, Sebastian," Anna ordered, and he keened, and Pia watched as Anna held on, pushed right to the edge of what she could bear in order to take him that much higher.

Pia was so close, her *please-please-please* a counterpoint to the heaving pressure that Farleigh was now exerting through all of them, his force reverberating into all four bodies that had become one.

"Please, Anna!" Pia screamed.

"Yes. Now, Pia," Anna whispered.

When Pia flew apart, it affected them all in different ways. Pia's fingers gripped and pinched Anna's small breasts, which she knew would multiply the intensity of Anna's release. Sebastian moaned desperately while Anna rode his cock through her orgasm. Farleigh roared to high heaven as he rammed into Sebastian again and again, pushing all of their orgasms higher and higher along with his.

"Now, Sebastian," Anna gasped.

And dear, dear Sebastian. Pia watched Anna's teary eyes as the man cried out a release that took him beyond the earth. His back arching beneath her, his strong arms fighting against the restraints, his head tossing and sucking the inside of her thigh desperately, all as he thrust up into Anna and then landed back down to take in Farleigh, again and again in a seemingly infinite circle of pleasure.

Pia slid away from his face at last, wilting from the consuming pleasure. She curled up near Sebastian's hip so she could watch as Farleigh's cock pressed into the other man's body.

Anna fell forward, keeping Sebastian's cock tight within her while he was in the last throes of his release. Pia traced Anna's smooth back as she rested along Sebastian's torso and kissed him tenderly.

While Anna kissed Sebastian, Pia leaned up to kiss Farleigh. Sebastian sobbed out his final glorious release, and Anna kissed him greedily, probably tasting their mingled scents, and she kept telling him how much she loved him, between those wet, messy kisses.

All the while, Farleigh kept kissing Pia until Sebastian shivered and bucked when Farleigh's cock finally slid out of him. Pia didn't want to stop kissing Farleigh, but he pulled away gently, caressing her cheek and helping her settle back among the pillows.

"Oh God," Sebastian whispered, beyond any other words.

Chapter 32

They all lay there for a spell, kissing and melting and petting one another for what felt like hours. Farleigh undid Sebastian's restraints and massaged the blood back into his hands. Anna stayed draped across Sebastian's spent body, with her right hand mindlessly caressing Pia's breast. Pia lay on her back, arms extended in that feline way of hers. Perhaps because she had been raised in a confined world of deprivation, she now relished even the simplest physical luxuries—like stretching—with an all-consuming appreciation, Farleigh thought.

He began moving around the tent, setting things in order, when Pia spoke, "Come, darling. You've been apart from us for too long." Her long arm extended elegantly, inviting him into the lovers' fold. Sebastian and Anna were dozing next to her by that point.

He looked up from where he was kneeling by the trunk a few feet away, and Pia must have seen that his eyes were shining.

"What is it, love?" she asked, concern in her voice.

He hung his head. "I don't know," he whispered.

She extricated herself from Sebastian and Anna, and she smiled when the other two hummed into a deeper sleep. Walking the few feet to where he was still kneeling, a look of worry crossed her face. Did she regret agreeing to marry him, especially under such extreme circumstances? She knelt down next to him and touched his shoulder lightly with the palm of her hand. When he relaxed into her instead of flinching, she squeezed his upper arm harder. "What is it, Leigh? Anything you want is fine, you must know that. Anything. We have no rules."

When he turned to look into her eyes, he felt exposed and raw. "Do you know what it is to want something, to crave something so deeply?"

"Yes," she whispered, touching him lightly, encouraging him.

"But then you know it's impossible. It's something society or humanity or the universe will never permit. So you spend a lifetime convincing yourself that your dreams are . . . impossible. That you are not allowed to have those dreams. Maybe little pieces of them, but never the whole dream."

"I know," she whispered. "We all three know what it is to feel like that, love. To want something and fear you are not only wrong to wish it but perhaps even damned."

He nodded.

"But you have bucked convention all your life. You have your title and wealth and the freedom that grants. What dream have you ever been denied?"

He looked across to where Sebastian was coming partially awake, with Anna still sound asleep against his chest. Sebastian's smile was a slow, dreamy hello.

"That," Farleigh whispered. "Look at him."

Pia turned to see Sebastian's angelic smile and continued to watch until his eyes drifted shut again. She turned back to face Farleigh. "He is a beautiful person."

Farleigh smiled and shook his head. "I know."

She reached under his chin to force him to look at her. "And so are you. That's it, isn't it?"

He nodded. "I don't deserve what you three have. I am not—"

She leaned in and kissed him, rough and biting. She didn't stop until he was nipping her back and they were both a little breathless. "That's better," she said. "We shan't have any of that unworthiness nonsense this late in the game."

But he felt his smile fading again. "When you spend your whole life convincing yourself of one thing, it's hard to let it go in a single afternoon."

Pia smiled. "Well, as you said, it's going to be a very, very long afternoon, isn't it?" His smile returned, but her brow furrowed. "Then again, if any of this has to do with you regretting asking me to be your wife, I shan't hold you to it—"

He grabbed her this time, both hands digging into the turn of her shoulders. "No! Regret? No. I'm in awe. I thought you were regretting it. I can't believe it even makes sense. I can't believe you said yes. It *doesn't* make sense!"

She smiled and leaned down to kiss his hand where he
tight enough to leave a mark. "Nothing of any real importance
perfect sense, does it, darling?"

He leaned in and kissed her again, hard and loving.

After he stopped, she looked confused for a moment. "So, I will
be a duchess?"

He smiled and shook his head. "I knew you were a scheming
wench at heart!"

"How far-fetched that sounds! Me! The very plain, very
unremarkable Patrizia Velasquez Carvajal, a scheming wench."

"You are no longer plain or unremarkable, my dear. If you ever
were to begin with."

"When you look at me like that I almost believe you."

"And how do I look at you?" he taunted, letting the backs of his
hands toy with the tips of her full breasts.

Her voice was getting rough. "You look at me like I am dark and
earthy and strong."

"Quite so . . ." He squeezed one nipple, hard, and she closed her
eyes and rode the piercing sensation. "Come with me," he ordered,
low and sure.

She followed him out of the tent, wanting nothing more than to
be taken by him the way he had taken Sebastian. Once they were out
in the clearing, she turned, breathless, to face him, expecting a barrage
of roughly barked orders that would culminate in Farleigh slamming
into her.

Both of them stood there, naked as babes, but instead of a sensual
attack, Farleigh dropped to one knee and held her hand in both of his.

"Patrizia Velasquez Carvajal, will you do me the great honor of
becoming my wife? Will you be the mother of my children? Will you
love me—and Anna and Sebastian—as long as we all four shall live?"

Her insides caved at the unaccountable tenderness and sincerity
of his proposal. She dropped to her knees and pulled him into her
arms. "Yes, Farleigh. Yes yes yes." She pulled at his hair and kissed
him hard. Within a few seconds they were a tangle of arms and legs

and lips and tongues. She scratched at him and watched his blue eyes darken with desire.

"You want to fight me, Pia?"

"Yes," she hissed. She breathed out of her nose, like a beast. "Don't you dare hold anything back from me, you promise?"

When he leaned down and bit the tip of her breast, she let out an aching cry. He dragged his nails down the center of her chest, along her smooth stomach. With his other hand he grabbed her wrists together and held them above her head. She arched up toward him.

"You want me to fuck you like I fucked Sebastian, don't you?"

She whimpered and nodded her reply, crying out again when he began to play with her arsehole as he said all those filthy things, hot and close to her ear.

"Alas . . . I think I'll fuck you properly first. All that begetting an heir and whatnot." He pressed his cock against her pussy, and she begged with a string of Spanish gibberish for him to take her. "Because a duchess must do her duty, isn't that right, Duchess?"

"Oh God, fuck me, Farleigh! I beg you!" she cried out in her thickly accented English.

He reared back and laughed. "You are the perfect duchess for me, Pia. Begging to be fucked. Is this what you want?" He pushed the head of cock harder against her wet, swollen pussy.

She tried to lift her hips to take him in, but he shoved her hip back against the soft grass. "You'll take what I give you, when I give it."

"Yes, Your Grace," she purred.

He smiled at her feigned compliance. "You will fight me, won't you?" She didn't know if he was exacting a promise or stating a fact.

"Yes, Your Grace." She bucked up against him again.

Pushing her arms even higher above her head, he growled, "Watch me, Pia."

She tried to focus her attention, but it was difficult as she was already slipping into the pleasure of his domination. Straining her neck up, she dipped her chin to her chest and watched as he entered her—until she couldn't watch any longer, the sensations and power of his movements pressing cries of joy out of her burning throat. He pounded into her, holding nothing back, transporting both of them to a plane of physical and spiritual union. He finally spent himself inside her on an animal cry of satisfaction, matched by her answering shout of pleasure.

Instead of loosening his hold on her wrists, he squeezed even tighter. "We will do very well together, I think."

"You think?" she said on a sigh, her eyes closed, her body pulsing with bone-deep fulfillment. He withdrew slowly, then relaxed alongside her, settling his strong protective arms around her.

"Yes. That's what I think." He began to breathe more evenly as she felt the cooler hint of early evening begin to creep around them. "Come. Let's go back into the tent so we don't catch a chill."

He helped her up, and they walked, holding hands, back into the dim tent. Sebastian stirred when they entered and lifted the sheet to make room for them. Pia slid in next to Anna and reached up for Farleigh to lie behind her. He joined them—truly joined them—at last.

Draping one large, possessive arm across the other three, Farleigh entwining his hand with Sebastian's to form a sacred union around the women.

"Home," Farleigh whispered.

And each of them agreed in their turn.

Home.

Chapter 33

Mandeville House, Gamlingay, England – One year later

Pia looked down at the baby suckling at her breast, then toward her beautiful husband and lovers. Farleigh was sitting on the couch a few feet away, reading a book while running his free hand languidly through Sebastian's hair. Sebastian was on the floor playing with one of the new puppies, his shoulders resting between Farleigh's legs. Anna was at the desk writing a letter to Isabella and Javi about their upcoming visit to England.

The four of them had spent the evening at a lengthy dinner with several neighbors, along with Farleigh's mother who was visiting from London. The dowager duchess had returned to her house on the southern end of the estate after the meal, but she was planning on staying in the neighborhood for the rest of the summer. She hated being away from her grandson for more than a few days at a stretch. Pia adored her mother-in-law, and the arrival of the baby had only served to solidify their attachment.

As much as she might love the dowager duchess, though, Pia loved the three people in this room a hundredfold. All four of them enjoyed being in company—they'd all laughed at the vicar's silly tale about his runaway guinea hen, and Sebastian had played a beautiful piece on the piano in the music room afterward—but it was always a welcome relief when they could retire to their private drawing room and be at their ease with one another.

When her son was finished eating, Pia adjusted her bodice and kept him in her arms. She loved to watch Edward sleep in that wonderful way so particular to happy infants: with complete abandon. When she looked up, Anna was standing up from the desk and trying to stretch her back. Pia smiled as Anna grumbled at the discomfort and inconvenience of being eight months pregnant in the middle of August. Whereas Pia had spent her entire pregnancy feeling like her body was finally embarking on its greatest purpose, Anna had declared she felt as though she'd been invaded by an army of Huns.

"This baby had better thank me!" Anna complained.

Pia shook with silent laughter so as not to wake Edward. "I'm sure he'll be entirely grateful, love."

"He? I'll probably have a cruel girl like myself, as some sort of divine punishment."

Sebastian looked up adoringly. "I would cherish a baby girl who was exactly like you." If such a thing were possible, Sebastian appeared to love Anna even more now that she was round with his child. "And then a boy and another girl and another boy—"

Anna covered her ears. "Sebastian! Darling! You must not torment me. The mere idea of all that reproduction is complete *torture*!"

He smiled at the word.

"Not that kind of torture!" Anna chided, but she smiled and walked toward her devoted husband. "I hereby declare that Pia must have all the babies in this family from here on out."

Pia laughed and then shook her head in joyful wonder. She felt the most delicious tingles run through her when Anna referred to the four of them as *this family*. "I would, you know," Pia said on a contented sigh. "I would love to have your babies, Sebastian."

Sebastian looked at Pia and smiled. "I would love that, too."

Farleigh looked at Anna and opened his mouth.

"Don't even think about it, Farleigh!" Anna snapped.

They all four laughed, and Anna collapsed on the couch between Pia and Farleigh. She was in such a state of frustration, Pia almost felt sorry for her. But not quite. Since Anna was always in the habit of rushing and managing and controlling, it was delightful to see her finally brought to heel by six or seven pounds of new life in her womb. She was subdued in a way Pia found enchanting.

Anna rested her head on Pia's shoulder. "I'm so *tired* all the time. How can you stand it?"

Pia kissed her cheek. "I felt so peaceful. I didn't feel tired. Now I feel . . ." Pia looked around the lovely yellow room in the beautiful country manor where the four of them lived with the new baby—and soon, the second baby. They were building a profound life together, a future. "I feel so overarchingly grateful. We're so lucky. And I don't want to dilute a moment of that with the slightest hint of bitterness."

Anna sighed and shut her eyes. "You always make me feel better, Pia. How do you do that?"

"I love you, I suppose, which helps." She reached her free arm around Anna's narrow shoulders. "Come. Rest with us."

Anna smiled and snuggled closer to Pia and the baby. "This is nice."

"It is," Pia agreed.

When Anna had fallen asleep completely, Sebastian stood up quietly and lifted her into his strong arms. "I will carry her upstairs to her private room to sleep, then join you both in the master suite?"

"Of course," Farleigh answered with a promising look. "We'll follow shortly."

Sebastian nodded and turned toward the door. Pia smiled when she saw Anna's delicate hands wrap lovingly around Sebastian's neck. *Poor lamb*, thought Pia. *She really is exhausted.*

After the other two had left, Farleigh moved closer to Pia and the baby. He reached out to touch one gentle finger along Edward's silky hair. "He is a lovely child. I'm so glad he has the set of your lips."

Pia smiled. "You enjoy willfulness, then?"

"It's not willfulness exactly. It's more of a persistent gentleness." He looked up into her eyes. "I can't help but feel that none of us would be here if it were not for you, sweet Pia. We're all selfish and stubborn and willful, and you . . ."

"Oh, I am also selfish, in the end."

"How so? You are always so equable and kind."

She reached up and touched his cheek. "Because this is what I've always wanted. All of us together, living as a real family. In my way, I have pushed for my selfish desires as much as anyone. Perhaps more so."

Farleigh leaned in and kissed her gently on the forehead. "Well, then, perhaps you are better at letting us *think* it's our idea, that we are getting our own desire."

She blushed. "Perhaps. And if that is the case, perhaps you are having the idea right now that you want to carry this baby up to the nursery and hand him to his nanny and then return to our room to make ravenous love to Sebastian and me."

Narrowing his eyes, he touched the turn of her ear, sending a shiver down her neck. "You see, that was *exactly* what I was thinking. You must have the gift of second sight."

"A very selfish second sight," she added, placing the baby into his arms and standing up to see herself out of the drawing room. Smiling over her shoulder, she gave him a saucy wink as she headed in the direction of the large master bedroom—and bed—they all shared.

Dear Reader,

Thank you for reading Megan Mulry's *Bound to be a Groom*!

We know your time is precious and you have many, many entertainment options, so it means a lot that you've chosen to spend your time reading. We really hope you enjoyed it.

We'd be honored if you'd consider posting a review—good or bad—on sites like **Amazon, Barnes & Noble, Goodreads, Twitter, Facebook, Tumblr,** and your blog or website. We'd also be honored if you told your friends and family about this book. Word of mouth is a book's lifeblood!

For more information on upcoming releases, author interviews, blog tours, contests, giveaways, and more, please sign up for our weekly, spam-free newsletter and visit us around the web:

Newsletter: tinyurl.com/RiptideSignup
Twitter: twitter.com/RiptideBooks
Facebook: facebook.com/RiptidePublishing
Goodreads: tinyurl.com/RiptideOnGoodreads
Tumblr: riptidepublishing.tumblr.com

Thank you so much for Reading the Rainbow!

RiptidePublishing.com

AUTHOR'S Note

There were many factors that contributed to the ideation and execution of this book. Writing hot sex for its own sake is fun, of course, but I also wanted to write about a time in history when homosexuality, bisexuality—really *all* sexuality—was not perceived in the binary context under which we now (I think) suffer. These imaginary characters have no such cultural paradigms to contend with. I believe in a broad spectrum of human attraction—both physical and emotional—and I am grateful this book gave me the opportunity to explore some of the nuanced permutations of that spectrum.

This morning, I was listening to a BBC Radio 4 podcast about David Hockney's *In the Dull Village*, and it summed up very nicely what I was trying to accomplish with this book: "[Hockney] felt a responsibility to stand up through his art for his own rights and to join the growing campaign for the rights of others like him. Characteristically, he was determined that his approach would not be heavy-handed. These etchings don't preach. They smile and they sing."

I hope this story smiles and sings for readers.

Megan Mulry
November 11, 2013

Acknowledgments

Sarah Frantz's editorial direction was an integral part of this story. I loved working with her at the happy intersection of our interests. The opportunity to discuss welts, Wellesley, and wedlock all in one email does not come along very often. I am also grateful for early reader feedback from Magdalen Braden, Anne Calhoun, Shelley Ann Clark, and Janet Webb. Lastly, I am so honored that Pam Rosenthal took the time to read and comment.

ALSO BY
Megan Mulry

ABOUT THE Author

Megan Mulry writes sexy, stylish, romantic fiction. Her first book, *A Royal Pain*, was an NPR Best Book of 2012 and *USA Today* bestseller. Before discovering her passion for romance novels, she worked in magazine publishing and finance. After many years in New York, Boston, London, and Chicago, she now lives with her family in Florida.

Website: meganmulry.com
Goodreads: bit.ly/1boncLy
Facebook Page: on.fb.me/1e3LYVL
Pinterest: www.pinterest.com/meganmulrybooks
Twitter: twitter.com/MeganMulry
Email: megan@meganmulry.com

Enjoyed this book? Visit RiptidePublishing.com to find more erotic historicals!

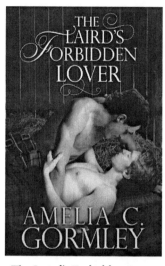

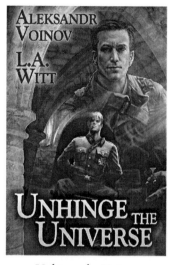

The Laird's Forbidden Lover
ISBN: 978-1-62649-020-8

Unhinge the Universe
ISBN: 978-1-62649-047-5

Earn Bonus Bucks!

Earn 1 Bonus Buck for each dollar you spend. Find out how at RiptidePublishing.com/news/bonus-bucks.

Win Free Ebooks for a Year!

Pre-order coming soon titles directly through our site and you'll receive one entry into a drawing to win free books for a year! Get the details at RiptidePublishing.com/contests.

CPSIA information can be obtained at www.ICGtesting.com
Printed in the USA
LVOW13s2136270514

387527LV00004B/390/P